HOT SCORES

A Joe Oaks Novel

Also by Bud Connell

The multi-award winning thriller
Peak Experience: A Novel

The thriller Peak Experience will rivet you spellbound as a financial monstrosity and the tentacles of international subterfuge become as plausible as the lead stories in today's headline news. This award-winning novel is available on Amazon's Kindle and all electronic devices using a Kindle App. The printed book may be obtained at Amazon.com, TowerBooks.com, Books.Google.com, BarnesandNoble.com and from other online retailers worldwide.

Excerpts from Reviews

Taut, tantalizing and terrifying!
–Susan B. Stroh, California, USA

This is a thriller that delivers. Enjoy!
–Ann Becker, Wisconsin, USA

It was everything I look for in a book.
–Tallahassee Lassie, Florida, USA

A riveting tale of intrigue and big corporate corruption.
–Don Logay, California, USA

Once you start, you can't put it down!
–Booklover, Ontario, Canada

HOT SCORES

A Joe Oaks Novel

BY

BUD CONNELL

PUBLISHERS

PUBLISHERS

ARC Publishers, and the ARC symbol
are service marks of ARC Publishers

www.ARCpublishers.com

Cover design by Bill Young Productions • Houston

TPB – Trade Paperback Edition
ISBN-13: 978-0615593708
ISBN-10: 0615593704

ACKNOWLEDGMENTS

Thanks to my friends and acquaintances in the radio and music businesses for contributing aspects of an offbeat backdrop for this hapless comedy-adventure and love story; and thanks, too, to other friends in Los Angeles and Miami for their input and guidance.

A special acknowledgment to Jim MacKrell, a guy with great story sense who provided motivation for the initial segment in the Joe Oaks saga, and a tip of the hat to Bill Young and Brian Love for their outstanding graphics and cover art.

My thanks, too, to my son John for his words of encouragement, and to my sisters Vicki Speck and Susie Brown (authors of Going Hog Wild with Country Cooking, one of the most useful little cookbooks on the planet) for their frequent query, "When will the first Joe Oaks story be finished?"

Here is Number One; and there are eleven more in the pipeline.

Table of Contents

Table of Contents (continued)

Table of Contents (continued)

And so we begin –
Joe Oaks

1 – Still Dressed Up in Fur?

I mounted the ornate barstool and ordered my usual high-ticket bourbon neat with an icy 7-back. Thirsty I was, and my tensed-up muscles needed a liquid massage after a bumpy ride in the Florida skies.

"Yo, Joe. You drank it all last week." Tylerfrank, my old buddy barkeep, stopped sliding glasses into the overhead rack, leaned down and stuck his face in my space. "I'll have to buy more stock with you coming in town every week."

"Do it, pal. I can't handle that cheap crap."

"Yer taste for good bourbon's gonna bite a chunk outta yer credit card."

"It already has, Bartender. Hush up and pour second best." Tylerfrank pulled a bottle from the booze rack and I felt the skin on my neck crawl. "Hey, that's Tennessee hooch. Pick another one."

"You got it, Joe-buddy." He chose a top shelf Kentucky medication that I hadn't yet tried and poured a double shot. I gave it a whiff, sipped a taste and smacked over it while he chucked ice cubes in a glass and filled it with chaser.

"It'll do, but it's not as good as my regular relaxer."

"Mr. Joe Oaks, you are a creature of habit."

I chuckled at Tylerfrank's peek into my black soul. If he only knew how many habits I had, the ones I wrestled with, and the ones I'd beaten down, mostly bad.

"Hey, that filly is coming in almost every day now." Tylerfrank started slicing limes on a cutting board.

"I can't keep track of all the quiff I sniff. Who you talking about?"

"The one I've seen you watchin'. She's coming in almost every day."

"Well do tell Rodelle, you *need* a little biz in this boozehole. I can't afford to pay all your frickin' bills." I thought for a moment. See, even Tylerfrank knows my bad habits, including the ones I try on the sly, like chickscoping. Hell, every guy does it. "Pour me another one. You talking about that good-looking rich blonde with the accent?"

Tylerfrank nodded. "Non other."

"No kiddin'. Still dressed up in fur?"

"Always. Like she's going to a Hollywood movie star party. She even asked about you a few days ago. Called you a nice man."

"I said hi a few times, never really talked to her."

"It looks like her door's open for business." Tylerfrank popped a rag at the round ass of his cute little waitress. She flashed her middle finger over her shoulder and skittered under the bar gate with her contraband corkscrew.

I took a long sip from the double shot glass and coughed, the warm medication seeping over my voice box and deep down into my gut.

Usually I notice what's going on around me, but that business about the rich chick was all new and welcome info.

I decided to hang around and see if she showed, and I resolved to slow down on the intake so I'd be sober or at least coherent if she came in. Tylerfrank said she usually appeared shortly after five when the trio started--three aging Miami Beach musicians who stroll around carrying their instruments and operating like they're playing to a frickin' full house even when there's only one or two lizards in the old hotel's fragrant lounge.

The Carousel, with its signature circular bar built like a merry-go-round, had been in the hotel since the beginning, so the story goes, and it smelled like it too. The Plage was one of the few hotels left from the early French Renaissance of the fifties, and it badly needed refurbing, but the room price was right.

And before I forget, the name Plage is like 'rouge' but with an *a*, and it's French for beach--the old Beach on the beach.

About the girl, woman; Tylerfrank said he thought she was Polish and used to be a supermodel. Yeah, it made sense. Katya Cahoone. A Polish supermodel married to a rich Irishman who owned more shit than the Vatican, and she asked about *me*. Holy crap.

2 – Hotcha for the Babe Auction

I waited for the gilded elevator on the phony black marble floor with flecks of gold in it, and that's when I saw her go into the lounge. She was a looker all right. Too short to be a long-term supermodel, but that's all right with me. I like 'em about an inch or two under my five-nine frame, and I do mean under it.

Katya what's-her-name out-looked the best of the two-hundred-dollar hookers I'd been picking up at the witching hour. Maybe if I played my hand right, I could save the two C-notes and have a quality piece of pound cake for tonight's dessert.

I took the elevator to my floor, unpacked and cleaned up, and noticed a little early gray showing through the black in my sideburns. So I got out the *Just for Men* and touched up. Might as well look like the young stud I am. I had to laugh at myself in the mirror, brushing forty and acting like a kid just out of school; but what the hell, I still could go all night with the right encouragement.

I splashed on a little *Cool Water* and I smelled hotcha for the babe auction. Maybe this was my lucky night, a freebee, if she was still there.

+++

The elevator door opened and I whiffed the horses' doovers that the hotel kitchen tossed into the lounge for the freeloading lizards. I'm one.

Screw the hundred dollar Miami Beach dinners. The only place they ever appeared was on my expense account. A high-flying, well-respected music promo man was expected to entertain. But *I* didn't. I didn't buy the greedy jocks all night feasts, or all night anything else.

Spiff, sniff and quiff, that's what the greedy scuzzes want. I give them the money and the small consumables, but I save the carnal benefits for myself. They can damn well buy their own skin and dinners with the free cash I dole for playing that rap-crap called music. Whatever happened to Frank and Dean? I'd even settle for some Hall & Oates about now. Good grief, Hall & Oates.

+++

The place was jumping. There had to be two, maybe three people at the bar, and a couple of tables were occupied with Miami Beach fossils. Tylerfrank was already off and replaced by a pair of young bored-looking brunettes in tight pants and low cut blouses. That was okay with me.

Katya, the goddess who asked about me, was nowhere in sight. So I ate a few hot wings and downed another double-shot as I looked around at the slim pickings. It was too early for the A-list to show up shopping for cash-paying Johns, or Joes in my case.

Anyway, I was shot to hell from spending all day in a puddle jumper saving airfare from California.

I went back upstairs, watched some shitty show about getting lost on some dumb frickin' island that I'd forget about by midnight, and fell asleep in my shorts.

In the middle of the night I woke, realizing the dream that jarred my eyes open was about her, Katya, the Eastern European supermodel crawling all over me. It felt good.

I smiled in the dark.

3 – Don't You Wanna Hear the Hits?

I got the morning out of the way in a hurry.

At noon, I met with Master Judd, the music director, and Willie and Romina, the morning hip-hop team on the leading FMer. Earlier I had stripped off nine brand new Franklins from my wad and slipped three of 'em into each of the jewel-cases containing this week's target hit. And here I sat in the witness chair in Judd's cluttered windowless office with stacks of shit all over the place; all looking disorganized and untouched for weeks and probably months. Willie and Romina sat to my right within reaching distance. I handed Judd the goods.

Judd snapped the case closed when he saw the cash. Same routine every time. Same ol', same ol', same ol' crap.

"Don't you want to *hear* the hits?" I asked.

"Naw, man. You're covered, that's cool." Judd passed two jewel cases to Willie and Romina who smiled and nodded, and he laid his, with the precision of a surgeon, in the middle of his top desk drawer, smiled at it, locked it in, stood up and said, "Let's go to lunch."

"I can't man." I lied. "I've got three more stations to hit before five." Bullshit. I followed him up out of my chair. I was done for the day.

"You coming back next week?" Judd asked.

"I doubt it. I don't get another raft of hits until the first of the month."

"You call everything you *promote* a hit, don't you?"

"As long as it costs nine bills to get airplay."

"I read, man--I read your brand of music."

"It's a good thing," I warned.

"Bye, Rachael Ray. We'll wait right here for your next recipe. Just bring the ingredients."

"Funny, real funny, Judd. See you in a couple of weeks." Jocks... all the same. Cross their greedy little palms with silver and they'll jump through frickin' fire hoops. Fail to show up with their car payment and they'll conveniently forget every hit you ever gave 'em.

I smiled to the skinny black receptionist, waved myself out the second floor studios and took the steps down two at a time. I had to buy a new shirt and shoes before cocktail hour. I intended to look like GQ when the subject of last night's dream date showed up in the flesh.

Yeah, last night I about destroyed the pillows, practicing.

+++

Later, feeling all spiffy, looking sharp and smelling good, I took my usual place at the bar. It was 4:45 and Tylerfrank poured me a double, which I committed to sip slowly while waiting for the attractive Mrs. Katya Cahoone to appear and carry me off to fantasyland.

She didn't show.

4 – My Florida Shell Game

"Well, kiss my ass, Sherlock." I slammed down the phone, flopped back on the bed and stared at the ceiling. No frickin' California lawyer's going to threaten me. New rule: never return a call to a frickin' lawyer you don't know.

When I turned in my used-up car, the leasing company tried to convince me that I owed more than I agreed to pay when I signed the dotted line. To hell with the greedy bastards. The car was finished, and so was the contract. Besides, as little time as I was spending in LA, I might as well not have a seldom-used vehicle sitting in Southern California covered with desert dust and cinders from canyon fires.

Sometimes I think ahead. I had already set up an account with a friendly little S & L in South Beach and called my California bank and told them to wire every last dollar. Later, I'd taken that money in a cashier's check and moved it to a small South Miami bank. If the ambulance chaser wanted to attach my funds, he'd have to frickin' find 'em first.

If I picked up a few more promo accounts, maybe I'd get that little black Mustang convertible I'd been admiring. I'd rent it in Miami and drive it back to LA over five or six days, and turn the whole thing into a road-trip vacation.

I dunno though. Six days on the road alone--

That's when I thought of that sexy little East-European super model. I decided I wouldn't be taking any mini-vacations until I'd satisfied my burning curiosity.

5 – That Makes Us Two of a Kind

Next, I had to go to South Beach and score some dope, some good buds and a little blow for this afternoon's radio station. No cash, just good dope. The jocks at the leading alt-rocker didn't want folding green, they just wanted to feel good when they played my clients' records. Who could blame 'em? If I had to listen to that shit thirty times a day, I'd want to be doped up, too.

I fired up the hot rent-a-car, a spiffy little green Toyota something or other, and hot because the sun had been beating on its phony leather passenger seat for hours with the windows up.

When I got to the right corner in South Beach, Ramon was waiting. He never looked nervous even though at any given moment he might be carrying a hundred-grand in nose-candy and other negotiable shit.

I rolled down the window. "Get in."

"Put your money where your mouth is. Better yet, Joe Oaks, put your money *in* your mouth, zigzag man."

"Get in, Ramon, before I drive off and find another fuckin' dealer."

"You said the magic words." Ramon pulled on the door handle and slipped his skinny ass onto the hot leather seat. "Hot! Dammit man, don't you have air conditioning?"

"Sun's been beating on that side all morning." I slipped it in gear and headed down Collins. "You got the shit on you?"

"Always, dude." Ramon leaped up from his seat and frowned at it like his eyes could cool it off. "Florida snow, aka foo-foo dust, and loooove weed. How much you need?"

"I don't *need* any. I will *buy* a grand's worth, the usual mix, and don't short me. I need as many lines as I can get. Okay?"

"For you, it's bonus day, Joe baby."

"Thanks, and thanks also to your crooked asshole suppliers."

"The babies in Colombia need new shoes!"

"I know who the babies in Colombia are. They're thousand dollar a night hookers who hang around your coked-up kingpins."

"How'd you get so worldly, Joe Oaks?"

"Knowin' dudes like you." I checked the rear-view for the all clear and pulled the car next to an unloading curb. "You better take this little envelope, there's ten crispies in it, and get out before some narc figures out what we're doing."

"I'm a no-narc risk. They're bought and paid for. When's the last time you heard of a South Beach bust?"

"I haven't."

"See?" Ramon gave me the okay sign. "Check your bag, jag. There's a little something extra to make your day go smoothly."

I looked inside. There was more hoot and toot than the usual order, and his *something extra*. I pulled out a small white envelope. "What's in this?"

"A handful of magic pills. Take 'em all at once and you'll write a dozen hit songs."

"I don't write music, I just promote the shit."

"Like me, I don't grow the dope, I just promote the shit."

"And that makes us two of a kind."

"I was thinking the same thing." Ramon popped open the door and leaped out on Collins Avenue and started walking backwards giving me the V for victory sign and winking as I shook my head and drove away.

Half my airplay depended on his crap, and if he were ever put out of business I'd be out of business, too, until I found another source. Crapoholic, that was something I didn't want to think about.

I tooled on across MacArthur Causeway, south on Biscayne and east into downtown Miami where the radio station sat on top of a seedy yellow brick building that badly needed sand blasting. It needed sand blasting on the inside, too, with the jocks and office staff still in it.

I deposited the dope and jewel-cases with Emeril Green, the director of programming, and Harold "Fat Baby" Wiggles, the music director, and they were all smiles. Good hash wasn't hard to come by in Miami, but reliable low-cut snow was another matter.

And for once I had enough left over to throw a minor party for two, if I wanted company in the endeavor.

Maybe tonight.

6 – If It's In the Groove...

On the way back across the causeway I let Norah Jones cut through my head and the warm Florida breeze waft through the car while I sucked in that clean Atlantic Ocean air. I felt good, more alive than I had in a long time. Even the palm trees that lined the little land-masses on the left and right looked healthy, not like the brown, emaciated over-tall transplanted sons-of-bitches in Beverly Hills––and that reminded me.

I steered with my knees while I punched in Kodi Graws' number on my cell. His answering machine picked up. Good. I didn't want to talk to the son-of-a-bitch anyway.

I listened to his outgoing message waste my time while I mentally rehearsed. *Finally*, a beep.

"Hello, Kodi. I left your Chickie-Dix CD with the station, and the music director said he'd give it eight plays a day for two weeks. That's more than you thought you'd get, right? Joe here, signing off. I'll give you another holler on Monday or Tuesday from Palm Beach." I cut off the ringer, snapped the cell shut and shoved it back in my pants, and took another deep pull of that fresh Atlantic sea air.

Kodi, my oldest client, when live on the phone, wanted to know too many facts and I ended up making up half the shit. I'm glad he wasn't in his fancy Rodeo Drive office.

Now his latest CD, that's a good one. The Chickie-Dix are a country girl trio, a crossover act in more ways than one, three butches, transsexuals who decided to become guys. Chickie-Dix, really--a California staple.

Most of my music promo moola came from record companies and producers out of Southern California, and I wondered if I could still get it if I based myself in the Sunshine State. Yeah. Living in Miami would be a different animal. Time to test.

I picked the cell phone out of my pants pocket again and checked the juice. Plenty. I pushed a button and said, "Manny."

I'm still amazed at how a little piece of plastic and metal crap can hear my voice and get somebody on the line three thousand miles away, and he'd know it was me calling.

"Hey, Joe. Whatchu want."

"A piece of ass, a pound of grass and a billion bucks. What do you want?"

"Did you get me some freakin' airplay?"

"I did, man, I did. So relax, if it's in the groove, it'll make its move."

"Records don't have grooves anymore."

"Who cares, shithead." I love this guy. "Hey, am I doing a good job for you or what?"

"Or what."

"Seriously," I emphasized.

"Yeah, you're doing a good job. Why?"

"Would you keep me on retainer if I moved my base to Florida?"

"I dunno, I guess. Hey, what about those freakin' Hurricanes?"

"What about those freakin' earthquakes? What about those freakin' fires, gangs, freeways, mudslides?" I was getting all red in the face.

"I was talking about the football team, asshole."

"--Oh."

"Who put a bug up your ass?" Kodi nailed it.

"I need a change."

"Obviously," he said in a smartass way; so I let his pause stretch out in kind of a smartass way too. "Yeah, I'll keep you on. But you'll be back."

"I know. Once a Californian, always a Californian," I said.

"If you're not working the LA stations I can't pay you as much as I do now." Shit. I dodged a palm frond in the middle of the road.

"Manny, come on. I'll work LA; I'll just do it from here. Same difference, airplanes go both ways."

Another long pause. "Okay dude, you're on. Just get me results. I need a hit bad."

"Done, daddy." I clicked off.

Before the end of the week I intended to firm up my current guys and have enough new clients to get out of Dodge and into the Florida beach life.

I brain-scanned through my New York and Nashville contacts, and made a mental hit list.

LA, my formerly favorite adopted hometown, had turned to shit. The traffic alone was enough to drive anyone completely crazy, and all the bad air rising up from the freeways into my nose yelled *get out* every time I was in town. On a drive into Burbank I couldn't pull in a deep breath and not cough my brains out. Psychological? I don't *think* so.

Besides, if I gave up my LA apartment and moved to Miami, the law favors the folks. It's a good place to escape if you got financial problems. I've heard there are more deadbeats per square inch in Florida than anywhere else.

Now, don't get me wrong, I'm not a deadbeat. I'm just a guy with a few loose ends--and I don't like to be hassled.

7 – I Love Your Rocks

The tables in the Carousel were nearly full but the stools were all mine. My buddy behind the bar curled a finger at me and leaned in close.

"She's here, she just went to the ladies room, and she's wearing a full length mink and covered with diamonds."

"Hoo hoo hoo. My time is coming, Tylerfrank. Where's she sitting?"

"Down there, end of bar, where you see the chocolate martini."

"Chocolate martini––that chick-pie does some serious drinking. Set me up with my usual adult beverage, right next to her."

"That's gonna look pretty obvious."

"Okay, make it one stool away."

"Better."

"Then I'll move over when I *recognize* her, with a huge surprise and a 'great to see you again' on my face."

"That works."

"Chu-yeah, I've done it a thousand times. Just different places and different faces."

I sat myself down and Tylerfrank slipped my double shot right up to my hand and the chaser real close behind.

"Here she comes," he said under his breath.

"That'll be the first time tonight, but not the last, booze buddy."

Tylerfrank shook his head and turned to the back-bar and replaced my bottle on the quality shelf. "Joe Oaks, you will never be cured."

"Who'd want to be?"

+++

"So you come to Miami Beach every season?" I couldn't keep my eyes off her rack. I swear I could balance a tray of longnecks on those puppies... and that Eastern European accent, double wow.

"January through April. I haff a penthouse next door at 7777. Well, my husbahn and I do. I like it here. I personally liff here almost year around." And I guessed without her husband nine months out of the year. She studied me like she wanted to lick my face.

"Is he coming in later?"

"He's in Europe."

"Bingo."

"What?"

"Uh, I said, you like bingo?" I almost blew it.

She curled her lip and cocked her head and looked at me funny like I was weird. "No, why?"

I had to think fast. "I know where there's a game and I thought you might want to win some money."

"My husbahn writes me checks." She pulled a long brown cigarette out of a red box and I scrambled for the matches and fired it up for her. "I don't even gamble when I go to Las Vegas. I cahn't keep track."

"Whaddya mean?"

"I cahn't keep track."

I think I got that. "What's he do?"

"Who?"

"Your husband."

"Oh. He's into lots of things. Mostly inports."

"You mean imports, importing?"

"Yeah, lots of things, but he rarely brings his business home."

"Too bad." God help me, I almost fell off the stool, I had so many comebacks to that setup, but she wouldn't have understood. *Does it detach at the crotch? Does he leave it in a jar in the office?* I almost busted a gut trying to hold in my laughing.

"Why are you vibrating? Why are you shaking? Why are you smiling like that? Tell me."

"I can't. It's something that happened today."

"Well, you could share."

"I will." Boy, will I share. "When I know you better."

"Well, I hope that's soon."

The opening. And there she was, all draped in mink and dripping with diamonds. I leveled one of my heavy ones on her.

"I love your rocks." Always compliment a woman.

"They're not real. I could get killed if I wore real ones."

"You could get killed for wearing those, they *look like* real ones."

"Yeah, but the joke would be on him."

Her puzzle was missing a piece, but what a beautiful woman. All that long blond hair with a slight curl all the way down to her ass.

I didn't know what else to say, so I just looked and listened to that accent for a while, and salivated--until it was time to move to the penthouse. When the cat's away...

"What brings you to the Carousel?" I reached an ashtray and slid it to her.

"We don't have a bahr in my building."

"I'll bet you have a bar in your penthouse, Mrs. Cahoone."

"Two."

I shifted my weight on the stool and waited for afterthoughts.

"By the way, please call me Katya." She looked me up and down. "Yeah, we've got two bahrs, but I don't like to drink alone."

"Neither do I, Katya. Neither do I."

8 – A Pat of Butter on a Hot Corndog

By one in the morning, the lady who doesn't like to drink alone and her new buddy from LA felt no pain. People came and went, and so did the Martinis and shots. I mean, I could have fallen off the barstool and broken my front teeth and both legs and I would not have known it. I'd have gathered up my stuff and shuffled out the Carousel on my nubs, dragging my legs behind me with Katya in her full-length mink on my arm while the rest of the shit-faced looked down and laughed. I mean we were that much out of it and I was that much into *her*.

"Take me home, Joe. I'm so drunk I can barely breathe."

"You said your husband's out of town?"

"Yeah, in Europe. He's gone for another week."

"What about the doorman?"

"He won't say anything. All you're doing is walking me to my door."

"He'll see me go up."

"Yeah, but he won't see you go down."

I didn't know what to say after that one.

+++

Katya is a raving beauty, for I'd say her thirty-five years. Maybe no mental giant, but what a winnerette. She even told me she likes the shape of my buns. Can you believe it?

Anyway, we slid off the stools, got our balance, scraped cigarettes and change into pockets and purse and I flipped a couple more twenties at Tylerfrank along with a friendly bird. He just winked.

+++

The 7777 doorman was nowhere in sight. Tonight the gods of sex, charm, and secrets were guiding me. I mean how lucky can you frickin' get?

Her building was new and filled with half-empty condos owned by New Yorkers. That kept the real estate at the high end of unaffordable and it looked like it, too. Especially when she slid the key in the lock and I pushed the door open. Talk about the French Renaissance, and Cahoone was Irish. There was more silver and gold and flocked wallpaper than in the A-room of the best whorehouse in France.

Everything came on all at once, the lights, the music, and Katya. She grabbed my buns with both hands and pulled me chest-first into her. Then she let go of my backside, brought her arms up and pushed my head down into her ample rack, breathing hard the whole time. Oh, mama!

"Are you gonna stay? Are you gonna stay? You have to stay!"

"You got a maid? Any help here?"

"They're off tonight."

And so was I, like a racehorse. I pulled her toward the nearest sofa. Clothes flew everywhere like backstage at a Rockettes tour. She pulled me down and before I could find my clubhouse pass, she started squirming to the side.

"Don't mash me, you'll bust 'em." That's all I need. Her old man gets home and she's got a frickin' flat front tire.

"No kissing, that means commitment," she said between heavy breaths and squeals. I was afraid the neighbors were coming, and they probably would if they could have seen the action in Katya Cahoone's living room. High school all over again.

"I'm so hungry. I'm so hungry."

"You shoulda eaten something."

"I will, I will."

She slid down me like a pat of butter on a hot corndog. That's not exactly what I had in mind, but it was better than okay.

+++

We laid there smoking–her pulling on her long brown cigarette and me on my normal Camel. She didn't say anything, but if she were ready for more, she'd have to go trolling at the Carousel again because I was drained--wiped frickin' out.

"You got to leave before seven. The maid is due at nine and sometimes she's early."

"Well, let's not take chances. I should leave tonight."

"Oh-h-h. I was hoping you'd hold me."

25

Julius H. Caesar, I'd found myself a beautiful rich wild woman who didn't want a commitment, and whose husband was in Europe. How lucky could I get?

9 – Joe Oaks, the Promo King

Workaday, workaday.

I started up the Toyota and planned my morning. Well, doo-wah-diddy; it was already eleven o'clock, so I planned my afternoon instead.

Get a burger and eat on the way to the radio station in Lauderdale. Tomorrow, Palm Beach. Make that West Palm, the low rent district. The closer you get to the beach, the higher the show ticket. Radio stations were not known for palatial palazzos.

First, I'd call Kodi Graws and give him a great report. And hit him for a raise.

+++

"Hell no, you sumbitch. If you haven't gotten Miami on it, I'm gonna can your ass."

"Johnson the Love Bulge turned it down flat." I thought it best to tell Kodi the truth, for a change. "But, Johnson said if I convinced his program director to add it to the general play-list on Friday, he'd play it for us like a deck of marked cards."

"Fair enough. You can stay on if they list it, and I do mean *if*, because the rest of Miami won't add it unless we got somethin' to show, and you better have somethin' to show by Friday."

"Kodi, I will, I will. I'll call you tomorrow afternoon with a good report." I hung up and blew out the breath I'd been holding.

Kodi paid well and I had to come up with an ace to make my fun-in-the-sun move; and I couldn't do without that big LA to Miami, Miami to LA expense account. No, sirree.

The name of the song was Naval Girl, about a chick on the sea working for Uncle Sam. Now, you'd suspect I'd be able to come up with some kind of promotion that would get a no-count program director to pay attention and put the song on his lousy station. Well, I didn't disappoint myself. I didn't get the reputation of Joe Oaks the Promo King for nothing. The answer was in my head before I stopped at McDonald's to take a leak.

The idea was simple, and it would bail me out of what could have been a jam-and-a-half, and it would keep me on my Florida moving schedule.

I dialed Katya's private number, the one that rang her closet. Yeah, she actually had a phone mounted in her walk-in closet. It looked like a frickin' clothing store and she said she spent more time in that closet and in her attached bathroom than anywhere else, and that the calls she missed were always transferred to her cell phone. Well, la-di-dah. When she told me that, I thought she had too much time on her hands. But if that's what it took to look that good, it was okay with me.

"Hello-oh." Her accent knocked me over every time I heard it. She could offer me anything and I'd buy.

"Katya, it's Joe. I got an odd favor to ask. Can you talk?"

"Sure. By the way, last night was super-fragilistic-ex-p, ex-p–whatever. I can barely walk."

"Would you loan me your mink coat?"

"Are you crazy? Whatever for?"

"A promotion. I need it for the afternoon."

"–I dunno. And it's a sable. Tell me more."

I couldn't tell her I was gonna put a naked hooker from the Carousel in her drop-dead coat. But if she'd loan me the rag, I'd save at least a hundred on a rental.

"I'm hiring a model to wear it into a program director's office, we close the door, she opens her mink coat and voilà, she's wearin' nothing but a CD called Naval Girl, taped to her belly. Whaddya think about that?"

"Cute, but it's a sable, Joe." She sounded genuinely impatient, almost angry. "Why don't you hire *me*? I used to be a model, you know. A good one."

Well, doodle me, I hadn't thought.

"How much would you charge?"

"For you? Nothing. My husbahn writes me checks."

I ran a brain tally. I'd save two hundred plus the hundred coat rental. Am I a good promoter or what? Charge fifteen hundred for a low-cost promotion and get three hundred in expenses free. All profit. The Promo King strikes again.

"You're on. I'll pick you up at ten in the morning and we'll drive up to Palm Beach." She was game for everything. "Katya, did anyone ever tell you you're one helluva woman?"

"Yeah, several times."

I could believe that. "Well, they beat me to it," and they probably beat me to a few other things.

"Oh, Joe?"

"Yeah?"

"This morning one was a little smaller than the other."

"One what? What do you mean?"

"I think you mashed me too hard lahst night."

10 – Why Don't <u>You</u> Rub It Off?

She met me in the 7777 garage by the elevators, she said, to "avoid the doorman". Safe and smart move. And there she was in her full-length mink glory; make that sable from head to toe. I couldn't help wondering if she was already naked as a hairless Chihuahua underneath all that fur. And, I'd had the Toyota all washed and vacuumed and it looked like a new dime.

"I'm not riding up there in that piece of… in that thing!"

"Why not, I'm on expenses."

"I don't care. I've never been in a Toy-yoder."

"Toyota."

"Whatever."

"We'll take the Bentley." She pointed over to the far corner where a cobalt blue bomb sat ready to be detonated with an ignition key. A queen's ride-in-waiting.

"Sure, if it makes you happy."

I parked my car in a guest spot and walked my lady toward her carriage.

"You're driving, aren't you?" I was sure she wouldn't ask *me* to get behind the wheel.

"Me? No, crazy? Me drive when there's a man around? I don't drive right-handed anyway."

"Well, *I'm* right-handed. What does being right-handed have to do with driving?"

"The steering wheel, Joe. It's on the right side, like in England."

I stopped and stared at the inside of the sedan and I started to feel detached at the brain. Crap, right-hand drive. "Let's take another car."

"Mercedes is at the airport. Darragh, my husbahn took it."

"Let's go in the Toyota."

"I won't ride in that… thing."

I took a deep breath and reoriented myself. I had to get to Palm Beach or I was gonna lose Kodi as a client.

What the hell, I might never get another chance to drive a Bentley with European plates; but if the program director sees it, his price to play the song would go as high as a giraffe's nuts.

I helped her in, fired it up, screwed around with the seatbelt and pulled out onto Collins. Before I knew it, I was doing 15 in a 30 and scared shitless. Cars were passing me right and left and I felt like I was on another planet. When I turned onto the causeway I moved it up to 25 in a 60, and by the time I got up to speed on the I-95, I registered a cool 40. People were mad, horns blowing, fists shaking out their windows, and they were screaming four and seven-letter words at us when they sailed past.

Katya watched me with her mouth open. "Why don't you go faster? This car has 160 on the speedometer."

I didn't answer. I just tried to concentrate and gripped the steering wheel tighter until my hands turned white. It was like being made to play the piano with your feet. I held my breath and prayed.

"Are you dressed under that fur?"

"SABLE. I'm undressed, that's what you want. Isn't that what you said you wanted, nothing but the coat?"

"Right. Sorry." Crap. Keeping the car in the lane was hard, like having to write with your foot that never held a pen.

She continued to stare and screwed up her mouth. "Are your *scared* of this car? Are you holding your breath? –Talk to me!"

"I gotta concentrate."

+++

It was white knuckle time and questions all the way up the I-95 and into the parking lot of the green stucco radio station with the little transmitter stick in the back on the outskirts of West Palm.

"What is *that*?" She pointed.

"It's a radio station."

"You're kidding? I got nude for *that*?"

I scratched around in my jacket pocket and pulled out a roll of two-sided tape and a jewel case. I removed the CD and handed it over to Katya.

"Here, tape this to your abdomen around your navel. Make sure it won't fall off."

"I'm gonna need help. I can't see below my, you know. I can't even see my toes unless I lean over."

I had to smile at that one.

"Let's get in the back seat." So we did. And in opening and closing all four doors of a three-hundred-thousand-dollar car we attracted the attention of a trio of pimple-faced young studs coming out of the radio station wagging CDs they'd probably won. They invaded the Bentley with openmouthed stares and I waved 'em off while trying to tape the piece of plastic called *Naval Girl* to the tanned belly of a gorgeous nude who'd doused herself in body lotion an hour before, but they got closer and kept looking.

"The tape won't stick, dammit. You're too oily— and you smell like nuts."

"Aloe vera and almond oil. It's not my fault I have dry skin."

"Right now you have greasy skin. It won't stick."

She reached in her purse and drew out a wad of tissues. "Here, rub it off."

"Why don't you rub it off?"

"I cahn't see."

God help me. I looked down and began to polish off the oil and cream from her bronze and beautiful skin and she started to moan. I was in frickin' trouble. I got a window full of teenagers peering in, and a hottie-in-heat, nude, in the backseat of a car that attracts more attention than a Michael Jackson trial. I was in deep trouble.

"Oh-hh-h, Joe!"

"Hold still."

"Oh—ohhhh. Oh-h-h-hhhhh, oh, Joe."

I got enough oil off and the tape finally grabbed on and held. Perfect. And, guess what showed through the hole in the CD, Mrs. Belly Button herself. Can you believe it?

I pushed the door open, flailed my arms and shooed at the little wiseasses. They scattered, jeering and pointing and panting like a herd of thirsty cocker spaniels.

"Help me out." Katya wrestled the mink back on. "Who are *they*?"

"Don't look at 'em, don't talk to 'em. They're just kids."

I pulled her out of the car and she overlapped the fur coat all the way down, covering up her assets; and we advanced into target territory, her taking small model steps to keep the coat from flopping open. I gotta admit, Katya looked good and she fit the bill for this gig.

"I'll get your silly CD played," she said.

I had no doubt.

11 – Playing It Just for Him

So we're standing outside the program director's office and I make the appropriate introductions.

"This is the famous European model, Katya." She nodded and smiled, gripping her mink up tight and close to her ample rack and concealing the glory beneath. "And this, Katya, is Howie Spins, the famous program director." Famous, like my ass.

"He's little, but he's cute." Katya ran her designer fingernail down his cheek.

Howie shivered and grinned ear to ear and flashed his set of ultra-whitened nipple-biters. I gotta admit Howie was a handsome little stud, all tan and blond and living on Florida sunshine.

"I'll play it just for him, Joe." Katya looked at me and pointed to the floor. "Wait for me here."

Arf, arf. She just commanded me like a dog and she was taking charge of the situation, which made me quite a bit nervous.

"Who's got the disk?" Howie looked at Katya and back at me.

I opened my mouth, but Katya filled in. "You'll see."

"Huh?"

She pulled Howie by the hand and kicked the door closed with the toe of her ultra-pointy stiletto leaving me standing in the hall.

Two minutes stretched to ten and the music coming out of Howie's office was so loud I couldn't hear what was going on, but suddenly I didn't hear any talking and I had the feeling they weren't dancing.

Just then, the station manager, a bulky guy with a shiny dome growing through a half-circle of brown hair came up behind me.

"What the hell is going on here?"

He didn't wait for my answer. He jiggled the doorknob and it was locked. So he reached in his pocket, pulled out a batch of keys and jammed the right one into the knob and twisted, pushing the door wide open all in one move.

Crap! My life was over. There was Howie's pants in a cloth puddle on the floor, and Katya, the bronze goddess, in her mink, sable, whatever, on her knees with Howie's shiny purple throbber in her hand. They both looked like they had seen the Second Coming, I'm certain they'd seen the first.

The general manager, Bob Burley, fired Howie on the spot and ordered Katya and me out of the station. All personnel had poured out of the offices and control room to see the source of the racket with Howie screaming at me for costing him his job.

"It's your fault, Joe Oaks. It's all *your fuckin' fault!*" It was the last thing I heard in our retreat through the exit as the screen door slammed behind us.

We got in the car and I was so rattled I couldn't drive, so I handed her the keys and she pushed 'em back at me.

Katya shook her head. "No, I'm too nervous. Besides he'll kill me if I scratch it.

"Geeze, Katya, you didn't have to do him!"

"It's your fault, you got me all worked up."

I shoved the key in the ignition and turned it, and the Bentley purred awake. The only sound in the car's cabin was the ticking from the dashboard clock and the fuse from the bomb called my life that would go off when I called Kodi Graws and told him what happened with Naval Girl. I could kiss off his two grand a month and the sweet expense account along with my move to Miami. Well, frick-a-doodle-do.

Katya sat silent and pouted and I pulled onto I-95 South. I ticked down what I'd say to Kodi and got lost in rehearsing what would be my final statement before I was sure Kodi pronounced the death sentence on me and my Florida plan.

I forgot I was driving from the right side and I let the big blue Bentley drift too far left and into the fast lane. That's when I heard the horn and Katya's one long squeal. A tag-team of blue-hairs on their way to Miami in a frickin' Cadillac Escalade and Mr. Cahoone's Bentley did a one-eighty on the Interstate like paired ice-skaters. Both cars stopped cold, dead, and blocking traffic for the better part of two hours.

Everybody was wearing seatbelts and nobody got hurt. Thank God, just paint scrapes and screeching brakes and a considerable set of dents, and lots of the wrong kind of attention.

Drivers and cops and mechanics from fire engines and police cars and wreckers, examined all occupants and vehicles, measured skids, wrote reports and pulled the two vehicles apart while I-95 traffic crawled along and every son-of-a-bitch going and coming taking a long look.

My life as I knew it, was over.

But Katya was a big hit, especially when the TV cameras rolled. She opened the mink and flashed for Channel 5 News. Can you believe it?

When the reports were wrapped and the wreckers started loading the two cars, the police transported the blue-hairs back toward West Palm and I pulled out my cell and called a cab to take us back to Miami Beach. A Yellow was only blocks away and picked us up in a New York minute. We sat in the back seat staring straight ahead.

"Did you have to show your beaver for the Six O'clock News for Christ's sake?"

"It's a sable."

"Sable! I didn't mean the coat."

She shot me a blank. "He's going to divorce me and I'll need a career."

"As what?"

"I was once a model, you know. A good one."

The cops had my name and license number and I was as good as dead when her old man got home. I was also a dumbass. It wasn't Katya's fault. I should've never involved her.

"Katya?"

"Yeah, what?"

"When's he coming back?"

"Who?"

"Your husband!"

"Oh. Two weeks now. He called and said he had to stay in Europe, in Colombia another few days."

"Colombia? Colombia's not in Europe. It's South America."

"It is?"

Maybe, just maybe. I didn't know exactly how I'd do it, but I would. "Tell you what. I'll get the Bentley repaired, and also fix the old ladies' Cadillac. That way your husband will never know."

"Can you do that?"

"I can try." I had a little stash of cash. "Hell, it's the right thing to do," and that little bit of bravado committed my stash to an early death.

Katya looked relieved and she gave me a big kiss on the cheek. I deserved worse.

12 – My Beans on the Floor

We unloaded at 7777 and I got Katya situated upstairs.

I retrieved the Toyota and drove the long block back toward the hotel, thinking all the way. I parked, fished out my cell phone and rang Beverly Hills. Kodi didn't even give me a hello.

"You're off the freakin' payroll, fucker."

"Lemme tell you what happened."

"Save it. I already heard."

"Who told you?"

"Howie Spins. He said he was calling Billboard and spreading the word that you're a freakin' spaz."

"That's not fair. It just got a little out of control."

"A little, my ass. You're out, Joe Oaks. Goodbye!"

There you go, a ten-year relationship with a guy I more than half-liked, which is above average for the music business. Beans on the table had just been scraped off on the floor. My plans were down the tube.

Miracle of miracles. I'm sitting there holding the phone paralyzed, and Kodi is still on the line.

"Joe? –Joe, tell you what. You owe me; you owe me, fucker. You get Naval Girl on the Miami station and I'll keep you on, but this one's a freebee, okay? Okay, Joe?"

I caught a breath. "Yeah, good. Good, Kodi. Freebee."

"And no more nudes who give head in the station, okay?"

41

"Okay, okay, Kodi. Yeah. Thanks, really." I was stunned. He wasn't a bad guy after all. But, and it was a really *big* but. The only things that would get Naval Girl on would be speed dust and happy weed, and plenty of it--a lot more than I'd given the needy bastards earlier in the week. I'd have to lean on Ramon, and for this one, I was *not* being reimbursed. *Screw me.*

13 – A Deeep, Deeep Metalico

First on the Saturday morning hot-list was have the Bentley delivered to a first-rate body shop. I couldn't go to the Rolls dealer because they knew the car and its owner, and I didn't want Cahoone to kill me in my sleep or toss me into an alley with a tire tool shoved up my ass. Besides, the Rolls dealer would charge a frickin' fortune. I called Ramon.

"Precisely the Best Body & Paint. All they do is imports. They take care of my sweet li'l Porsche." Ramon said Emilio and Carlos ran the lowest-priced shop in town for expensive foreign cars.

Two hours later I'm in the shop and the two brothers, a couple of Cuban exilitos, walked around the cobalt blue Bentley shaking their heads and saying, "Too bahd, tough break, m-mmm-mm. Too bahd––too, too bahd. And look at theese wahn over heeere."

"Well, how much? How much to make it like new again?"

"Wow, señor, too bahd. It's a deeep, deeep *metalico.*"

"Can you give me an estimate, or what?"

One of the guys nodded and gave me a *patience please* two-handed gesture, and the other began to write on a clipboard while they gabbled in Spanish and pointed, first at a dent or scrape on the car, and then at a spot on the paper secured by a metal clip.

The process went on for what seemed like several hundred years and Emilio and Carlos stopped talking simultaneously. Emilio ripped the top sheet off the clipboard and smiled broadly, showing a prominent gold tooth.

"For you, señor, freend of my freend Ramon, a bar-gain."

I snatched the paper and my eyes glazed. $18,367.94 and that was for the Bentley. An hour later they finished estimating the Cadillac and it was a shade under ten grand.

I told Emilio and Carlos to keep the cars and go to work. Someway I'd cover the bill. I just didn't know how, but I was beginning to get an idea.

14 – Meathawk Over a Mouse

I called Fat Baby, the music director of the Miami rocker, to test the airplay water. He and Emeril Green, the program director, were gonna hold my head under and make me drown.

"Play that piece of crap? It'll cost you triple." That meant I'd have to go into the hole by multi-grand to score enough dope to get the CD on the station.

So, the upshot–I needed twenty-eight grand for the cars and at least another three for Ramon so he'd supply enough stuff for the Miami airplay and I could get my job with Kodi reinstated. It was not going to be easy. I put in a call and Ramon said he'd meet me at three on the usual corner.

+++

He hopped in the Toyota and I laid the beg on him.

"You're crazy, Joe Oaks. Say it again slow, you want me to do what, crazy man?"

"Ramon, come on. Just let me owe you."

"How much you got on you?"

"Uh--" I reached in my pocket and pulled out my wad. I counted off eleven C-notes. "I can't give you all of it."

"Give me a thousand. You can owe me the other two grand until this time next week. And I do mean, next week."

What if I didn't make it in a week? He'd kill me. "Give me a month, Ramon. If I save my job, I can keep buying. If I get terminated, you lose a customer for life."

"Hey, if you don't repay, you get terminated anyway, *comprender?*" I sat there, trying to get my head around the consequences of missing the deadline with Ramon watching me like a meathawk over a mouse. "Okay, three weeks. That's it," he said.

He hopped out, grinning and walking backwards and flashing the V-rabbit-ears with both hands, and leaving the goods in a snow-white envelope on the floorboard balanced up against the firewall. I looked at it a good long time before I pulled out into traffic.

A knot in my stomach, or more like a black hole bloated up into my consciousness.

So there I was. I had to come up with thirty big ones in three weeks, and most of it in seven days or less. Shit-house-mouse.

15 – A Tender New Bush

Sunday morning Katya was horny again, and that was okay with me. She'd let the maid off for the weekend and I was tired of sitting at the bar and having Tylerfrank ask me questions about her considerable talents. I noticed I had started to lie a lot anyway, because frankly, some of it wasn't any of his business. He did get one helluva hoot out of the Naval Girl story with Howie Spins getting fired and all, but I didn't find it all that funny. So as a recompense, he offered me more receipts.

"Here's one for $206 and some change. How about that? And here's a wad of good ones from last night. Marybella cleaned out her pockets." If I weren't so balled up with Katya and my pressing problems, I'd take a swing at that cute little brunette barmaid. Anyway, the extra receipts would help on expenses, but they wouldn't go very far in filling in my big ass shortfall.

I ordered another double and thought about my predicament until my Kentucky medicine took effect. Then I stopped ruminating and decided to show up early at Katya's penthouse. I brought a bottle of good wine and the love weed and few lines of foo-foo I'd been saving for a special occasion. With all Katya had been through with me on Friday, she deserved a good time. And it was almost Valentine's Day, so I picked up a big red rose and a box of Godiva chocolates, and it cost me thirty-nine bucks. Am I romantic or what?

+++

"Oh, you sweet thing!" Katya was all over me like honey on a bear's paw, and I gotta admit I was looking forward to our Sunday free of cares; especially after this week, which I'd just as soon forget ever happened. She pulled me toward the curvy couch and pushed me down on it, flopped down by my side and wrapped those pretty arms around my neck. I decided to let the action begin.

I leaned over on the ultra-modern white foo-foo sofa and hooked her around her waist and pulled her up closer to me.

"Oh, Joe! This is the nicest Valentine's Day I've ever had."

Well, that's all I needed. I leaned to the side and she collapsed under me like a tender new bush in the forest.

"Don't mash me, you'll bust 'em."

"I know. I know."

And the party began.

Katya let it all fly, and I was hoping the penthouse was soundproof. But I stopped thinking about all the noise and lost myself in the heat of the moment.

And Katya lost her accent.

"Oh, dammit, Joe, dammit, dammit, dammit. Don't–stop–Joe! Oh, golly, Joe-baby, do it deeper, do it deeper!"

That's when I began to suspicion she wasn't from Poland. After the second act climax we took an intermission and lit a joint, and I had to ask.

"You're not from Poland, are you?"

She took a beat and said softly, "Detroit."

"Figures."

"How'd you know?"

"When you get excited you lose your accent."

She made dimples and looked down at her rack. "I know, I lose it when I'm hot."

"How'd you learn to talk like that anyway?"

"An acting coach up in Hallandale."

"Well, she did a good job for the most part."

"He. It was a guy. I had to trade it out."

"That figures."

"He worked on me a lot," she said.

"And vice-versa?"

"Huh?"

"Nothing." Glorious Katya looked out the window at the skyline. She was a piece of work alright, a good girl. It's just her bricks weren't laid all the way up to her roof.

"What's your *real* name?"

"Katya!"

"I mean your *real*, real name."

"Poo on you, Joe Oaks. It's Catherine Lucille Bobo, and it's a real, real name and don't you make fun of it."

I almost fell on the floor, but I held back from laughing. Poor kid. Anybody from Detroit with the last name Bobo should definitely have imagineered a new name *and* a new background, even a Polish one.

She sidled up to me and nudged my neck. "You know, Joe. Nobody ever treated me so nice as you." That was sweet, and then she backed off, looked up at me and made dimples again. "I got a secret."

I couldn't imagine what it'd be. I just looked at her and raised my eyebrows.

She smiled and looked down, and brushed something imaginary off her rack. "I'm not really married. We just live together. I told him I wouldn't do it unless I could act like the Mrs."

Well, that little bit of news from my Detroit princess didn't really surprise me, and it didn't uncomplicate my life. "And he said okay?"

"Okay, he said, but only in Miami Beach. I don't travel with him. I'm like the Miami Beach wife and that's it."

Poor kid. I didn't know what to say.

"Aren't you gonna *say* anything?"

"I'm thinkin'."

"It kinda opens up the space for us, Joe, doesn't it?"

I looked at Katya, oh hell, Catherine Lucille Bobo, and I smiled back. I had to think this one out. It's like when somebody gives you an expensive pussycat that only eats caviar and you live in a downscale one-bedroom apartment and travel a lot. I mean there was no easy answer.

"Well, I'm going to open the wine while you do your thinking. Do you want a pizza? I've got some in the freezer."

The fat doobie made me hungry as hell. "Yeah, pizza's great." She winked and busied about through the door where I could see her, whistling and singing fractured lines from *My Fair Lady*. I just sat on the sofa and smoked and thought.

Then I heard a stove bell ding, and two minutes later Katya rolled in a cart with the pizza and a salad and the Merlot I brought. She was a good girl, and pretty handy in the kitchen.

We ate and drank and smoked another fatty down to zip and got into it again. She fired off more times than a row of howitzers and I was hotter than a dog with two dicks. I was falling in love. Oh crap, I don't think I said that. Did I say that?

Anyway, in the heat of humpery, one of us accidentally kicks the ashtray off the coffee table and I guess Katya's live one, one of her long brown cigarettes, rolled across the floor and into the bottom of a sheer drape. They should make that shit non-flammable. We were so busy burning up the sofa that we didn't see what was going on behind us until the end of the room looked like a Texas bonfire before an Aggies game.

I leaped up and Katya started screaming. The drapes went up like a Christmas tree in February and set fire to everything near the windows.

"Where's the phone? Where's the phone?" I was screaming louder than she was. And she couldn't find the cordless son-of-a-bitch, so there we are in the nude running around and bobbing up and down and screaming, and about to be barbecued.

After wiping all the stuff off the coffee table in a panic search, she jammed her hand between the cushions of the sofa and miraculously pulled out the phone and punched 911, and in all the confusion couldn't remember her own address so I yanked it from her and took over. After barking out the right info, they wanted to know who was calling and I stupidly yelled out my name. Good grief, how dumb can I be.

The flames went to the ceiling and Katya went into full panic mode, and that's when the sprinklers kicked on and wet down the entire room like a rain forest in June. Katya's big hair became flat, drippy small hair and we looked like we'd been caught in a Manila monsoon.

It was about then the Fire Department crashed through the door followed by police and building security, and both of us still butt-ass naked and running around like hysterical natives on hot coals.

16 – My Smoky Little Princess

Two hours later, whatever hot spots the sprinkler system didn't knock down, the firemen did, and the place was in shambles. The fire marshal performed the last task of the night, a detailed report and he kept sniffing the air and screwing up his face.

Katya was too upset to talk, so I took over and told him how it happened, leaving out, of course, all the juicy X-rated details. I hadn't yet begun to think about the problem this little event was adding to my growing disaster list.

After the cops, firemen, security and super left, Katya plopped down on the squishy sofa and cried.

I had to take charge. I pulled her up by her perfect little hairless arms and held her close to me. "Don't worry, baby. We'll get all this cleaned up. I'll take care of it."

"He'll know. I'll have to call the insurance company. He'll see the reports. He'll kill me."

"No, no he won't. You won't have to file a claim. I'll get it cleaned up before he gets back. It'll be like it never happened." I hoped, and I'd need a Mother Mary-size miracle.

"Promise?"

"Promise." I didn't know how, but I would. "Call one of those fire damage clean-up companies first thing tomorrow and get an estimate. And I'm gonna put you up at the hotel tonight, in your own room." It was the least I could do for my smoky little princess.

"You're an angel, Joe."

I smiled and sheepishly looked down at the soaked white carpet and the black boot tracks. God, I was beginning to like her too much.

But, I was no angel. I was a dumb son-of-a-bitch trying to save his ass from getting killed Mr. Darragh Cahoone when he got back in town.

No telling what he'd do to poor Katya, alias Catherine Lucille Bobo of Detroit.

17 – In My Guru Sort of Way

I got Katya situated in a Plage mini-suite on my own dime, and she was beat like a rug. I told her to take a hot bath and go to bed.

Katya stripped her house key off her key chain, handed it to me, kissed me on the cheek and hugged me tight.

"You are such a doll, Joe, for taking care of me."

I smiled to myself and patted her on her shapely bum-bum. "You take that hot bath now and get some sleep. Things will look a lot better tomorrow," I said in my guru sort of way.

She dropped her little hairless arms, backed up and collapsed on the bed. I doubted she'd make it to the tub. I leaned over and stroked her hair for about a minute and she closed her eyes. I could hear her breathing softly, so I pulled the chain on the bedside lamp and Mr. Softy backed quietly out of the darkened room.

Time to lift the tail of the old donkey and look it right in the eye--time to face reality. I headed back to the condo. Tonight I'd get a head start on the cleanup so maybe the tab from the professionals wouldn't hit me so hard.

I had squirreled away a few thousand for emergencies, and this was certainly an emergency of the highest order. The ol' Joe Oaks commitment to what is good and right would come through once again.

18 – *Looking at the Long, Long Green*

Feeling the need for a little pick-me-up, I shuffled into the Cahoone kitchen and looked for coffee, found it and made myself a cup; and sipping it, moved around through the spacious palazzo surveying the damage, and snooping, as is my custom, into areas that were non of my frickin' business.

The firemen had forced open Cahoone's own locked den, or I'll call it a library, since it was full of books and other depressing crap. I entered, careful not to spill coffee on Cahoone's frickin' Oriental rug, and I moved around behind his desk which was locked up tighter than an old maid's douche bag. That's when I saw it.

The fire guys had apparently kicked open a small panel-like door behind the desk into a crawl space that served no particular purpose, except that it was full of small cardboard boxes that looked just alike, and I thought they probably had to do with Cahoone's business. Well, you know me and my curiosity. Katya said he was an importer, and I just had to see what it was that he imported.

I placed a box on the desk and carefully stripped the sealing tape off so I could put it back after I took a little look-see inside. Then I stood there like a concrete statue for about five minutes staring at the contents, my brain on full tilt.

I was looking at the long green. I mean the long, long green. Each box was about a foot long and almost a foot wide and six inches deep, and inside were eight stacks of new C-notes.

Now, if my math was ever any good, it was certainly most accurate when counting money. I riffled my finger down a stack of bills and could estimate that each stack contained a hundred thousand dollars. Holy Jack and his brother, I was standing there looking at a little brown box containing eight hundred grand; and thirty-five or forty of the little bastards just like it stared back at me from the crawl space.

Whatever Cahoone did, he was successful at it; but assuming all the other boxes were the same, why was he hiding all this cash behind a fake wall?

The question burned like a branding iron, but it couldn't be answered. Besides, it was none of my frickin' business.

Hard as it was, I set my jaw, clenched my teeth, resealed the box, and put it back on the stack. Then I carefully replaced the panel and continued my perusal of the place, cleaning up what I could, sopping up a few water spots, and all the time thinking about all that cash stashed in Cahoone's office.

Thank God, the fireman didn't get as curious as I was.

19 – It Just Keeps Getting Deeper

"Smoke damage, Joe. It's everywhere! Even my sable got smoked." She was talking fast and half-crying. "All my clothes, and Darragh's too, have to be cleaned, plus the carpets. And repainting, and a lot of wood and the drapes replaced. Even the plastic plants melted!"

"So, what's the bottom line to get it back like it was."

"First they have to wipe the ceiling and wipe down all the walls to get rid of the stuff from the fire extinguishers."

"Give me the bad news."

"You don't wanna hear."

"Tell me."

Katya took her usual long beat and then blurted, "Thirty-four thousand, six-hundred and forty-seven dollars, and I'm sorry."

I had to let it sink in a few seconds before I could form words in my head.

"Joe, are you there? Did you hang up?"

"I'm here. And don't be sorry, it's not your fault." Oh, man, the shit just kept getting deeper. "Does that include the drapes and plants?"

"Yeah, everything. I'd help, but he only gives me checks for groceries, clothes, hair and makeup."

I tried to sound cool. "Tell 'em to start tomorrow."

"You're the best, Joe. You're a real doll of a man."

A doll of a man.

We hung up and I added the princely sum to my mental tally and got dizzy. I was up to sixty-five thousand, all command payments due in three weeks or less.

I could've told Katya to tell her fat-cat fake husband to crack open a little brown box and cover the damage himself, but that's not the way Joe Oaks was built. Besides, I was sure Katya had no knowledge of the cash cache, and I'd also made a commitment to her and that was that.

So, I spent the rest of the morning on the phone with New York, LA and Nashville attempting to line up music clients. There were only a couple who needed a good promotion man, and no one wanted me to start until the first of the month.

I'd have to pull one out of my tail, but I didn't like what I was thinking.

20 – Since I Provide Good Shit

My watch said one o'clock and I needed to get to Miami by two and deliver Naval Girl along with the goods that would get the airplay.

Fat Baby and Emeril Green were waiting for me in Fat's office.

Fat Baby spoke first. "Did you bring it?"

I tossed the CD on the desk and smiled.

"Screw that," Emeril said. "Did you bring the good stuff?"

"Yeah." I dug down deep inside my coat and dredged up the big white envelope that I had folded three times. It was thick, and I could barely get it out of my pocket. I handed it to Emeril and he looked inside and grinned all the way across his face.

"Looks like you scored." He pushed the envelope over to Fat Baby and Fat opened a small packet, wet his finger and tasted a touch. "You gotcher airplay, this shit is wild."

Then I decided to make my test-move. I knew they owned a warehouse and put on all-night parties. "Is there anything else I can help you guys with... if you know what I mean?"

Emeril leaned in like he was going to give me a stock tip. "Maybe, since you provide good shit." He leaned in further and whispered. "We're throwing a little for-profit rave and we need reliable refreshments. We need thirty grand in assorted fireworks."

Fat Baby rattled the envelope. "About the same mix as this, plus some XTC. Can you do it?"

I took a short pause and said, "Yeah, no problem." I wasn't sure I could get the stuff; but oh well, what the hell, I plunged in further.

"Cash now. That's the only way it works." I talked like I knew what I was talking about.

"Pick it up from Fat Baby tomorrow at eleven," Emeril said, "and bring the stuff with you."

Crap in a hand-basket. Now, how the hell was I going to pull that off? I only had one ace and wasn't sure I could count on it, but I took the shot anyway. I nodded the somber nod of the big-time dope dealer. Thirty-grand cash. Snap, just like that.

21 – *Spearing Foo-Foo Dust*

On the way back over the MacArthur Causeway I retrieved the cell and called Ramon.

"Yo, Joe. Whassup?"

"Gotta see you quick." Cut to the chase. "Available?"

"For you, yeah. Got my money early?"

"No. It's something else."

"No more credit, Joe-baby. Not till the first one's paid."

"Can we get together? It's important."

"–Yeah, three o'clock, usual place."

"That works." I snapped the phone shut and bit my lower lip until it almost bled. What the hell was I doing?

+++

When I drove up to Ramon's outdoor office I had like a softball in my stomach, which tightened into a small hard knot and then expanded, all over what I was about to say.

He hopped in. "Yer late."

"I almost didn't come, I'm having second thoughts."

"Sounds like *more* than spearing a little foo-foo dust for hungry noses." Ramon sure had a way with words.

I couldn't answer right away. I pulled out in traffic and drove about a block with him staring at the side of my head before I had the nerve. "Yeah. More. Lots."

His tone went wary, distrustful. "Are you about to stiff me?"

I had to fake indignant, so I made myself look all huffy. "No, Ramon. If I have to get a cash advance from plastic I'll pay your ass."

"So what izz-it?"

I had to build up to it to lay it out straight, but the pause lengthened until Ramon took a deep, noisy breath and looked away.

"Okay, one of my guys wants a thirty-grand care package by four today, he'll have the cash, and I want to make a few thousand off it. Got it?"

"Not a problem. A few thousand, no. I'll pay you what you owe me, but I go along to make the exchange. And no more credit. Is that it?"

"It's that." And here it came. "Plus, I want to start dealing."

"Fuck, man, howdya mean? You wanta push in on *my* action? This is my copping zone. Not a chance, pal." He was shooting bullets at me with his eyes.

"No, no. Nothing like that."

"Well, what then?"

"I want to make a big score quick."

"You want to import, you want to be a Barnes man?"

"I don't even know what a Barnes man is."

"Big dealer, like me but *really* big. That takes clean green man, and you owe me piggy bank change. So how you gonna come up with hundreds of thousands?"

"I'm not. I need to *make* sixty-five grand, quick. In two weeks."

"You're shit out of luck." Ramon squinted at me like I was some form of unknown fruit. Then he turned away and stared straight ahead at traffic for a couple of lights. "You need way more'n that to get into the game." He lit a cigarette and inspected me a long time out of the side of his eyes. "Explain."

"The guy's car I wrecked, I accidentally set fire to his condo and I have to fix 'em both before he gets back in town."

"Dammit, man! You *are* a frickin' accident." He reached up and pulled the seatbelt down and snapped it into place. Then he stared straight ahead and I stayed quiet for a half-mile.

"Freight agent."

"What?" I slowed down to concentrate on what he said.

"Mule… you become a mule. The big boys need guys who'll get the goods on shore, or over the border. That's worth big money. It's also big trouble if you get caught. Ten to twenty, or worse."

"How do I make a contact?"

He took a deep drag and blew part of it out. "I dunno if it's a good idea. I'll have to consult my up-line and get back to you."

"Up-line? What is this a fuckin' multi-level like Amway?

Nothing was said for two blocks, and then Ramon shook his head. "Joe?"

"What?"

"Don't mess with this shit."

I just looked at him. It's the only time I ever saw Ramon look worried.

22 – *He Licked Her Palm, No Kidding*

"Hey, Fat, get in the back." Fat Baby opened the door and plopped all four-fifty into my poor little rental. The Toyota sank about six inches and groaned.

Ramon, ear-ringed, purple-vested and tattooed, twisted around to face Fat in the back seat. "You got the thirty grand on you? Lemme see it."

"Who the hell are you?"

Ramon twitched and a tic came up like he was trying to blink something out of his eye, or get up nerve to kill somebody.

"I'm the fuckin' guy you wanna see, asshole. You want the dope, show me what yer trading for it."

Boy, that was the way to blow a deal, but I guess not. Fat Baby looked at me and I nodded. He pulled out an envelope about three inches thick, spread the opening wide and riffled his chubby thumbs across the edges of the C-notes.

Ramon's tic went away. "Okay then." Ramon leaned over and snatched the envelope out of Fat Baby's hand. "Gimme a tour first."

"Huh? Where's the shit, man?"

"You'll get it in a minute." Ramon patted his chest with both hands. "I never been inside a radio station. Gimme a tour."

Fat Baby looked at me again and I shrugged.

And then Fat shrugged, "Well, okay. But don't talk to nobody."

"Why? I'm not good enough to talk to yer frickin' disk jockeys? Eat another cheeseburger, fat boy." Ramon leaned up in the seat and stuffed the cash-filled envelope deep in his pants.

"Hey, you guys," I interceded. "Let's just do a deal and call it a day."

"I wanna see the radio station," Ramon insisted.

I started to tell him that we'd wait on that one, but Fat caved.

"Well, okay. But man, you look like a frickin' pimp."

Ramon steamed. I swear I could see it coming out his ears.

And you look like a fuckin' mound of crap from a big fuckin' elephant. Why don't you eat six more cheeseburgers?"

Both guys opened the car doors at the same time. I thought they were gonna roll in the dirt, but they started laughing and slapping each other's backs. I guess Fat wanted the dope and Ramon hoped Fat wouldn't sit on him.

I followed them up the stairs and they were talking like ol' buddies. Hell, I don't understand people.

At the top of the steps Emeril Green was coming down the hall toward us and he waved, but did a double take when he saw Ramon.

"Who's this?"

"Friend of mine," I said.

Fat tagged, "He's got a special delivery."

Ramon looked around and started walking toward a bullpen desk where a cutesy girl was pounding away on a keyboard. He yelled over his shoulder. "You promised me a tour first."

The brown-skin doll with a turned-up nose and short blond hair looked up. I'd seen Havenetta in here many times before, I think she did Traffic, which is figuring out which commercials go where; that is, whenever Emeril Green wasn't shagging her in his office.

"Ramon! Whatchu you doing here, baby?"

"Sneakin' up on you, bitch. Howz my favorite li'l dancer?"

She held out her hand and Ramon took it, turned it over and overtly licked her palm.

She shivered and squealed and looked down and moved her head from side-to-side. "You'll always be my first love, you sexy man."

It was then that Emeril came into her vision, barreling toward Ramon because, I think, it looked like Ramon was hitting on his doll.

Anyway, Emeril did a full body blow like a fullback tackle, and pancaked skinny Ramon down on Havenetta's desktop flat on his back. The two of them slid all the way across and down on the floor, taking the computer and keyboard and all of Havenetta's traffic crap with them, along with her Diet Dr. Pepper and lit cigarette and Ramon yelling all the way.

"You crazy fucker!"

The impact must've popped a plastic bag because the special delivery was being delivered.

A cloud of white dust billowed up around Ramon, and Emeril backed off and looked like he'd been hit in the face with a bag of flour. Polvo blanco and rasta weed and XTC tabs scattered all over the floor and we were all poppin' birdie powder even if we didn't want to.

"You're not supposed to be in here with that shit!" Emeril yelled louder than Ramon.

"You ordered it, you dumbass motherfucker, and you're gonna pay for it." Ramon pulled himself up using the edge of Havenetta's desk. "In more ways than one, you're gonna pay."

"You shouldn'ta been messin' with Havenetta."

"I don't see no 'Do not trespass' sign on her round ass, now do I?"

Emeril looked away 'cause Ramon had got him. Ramon had no way of knowing that his female friend was Emeril's fur pie.

"I'm sorry man. Let me help you get the stuff up." Emeril started picking up pills while Havenetta was crying in the corner.

"Help me, hell, you get it up. You bought it." And with that, Ramon started emptying his pockets; all of them except the one containing the thirty big ones; and pills and weed and foo-foo dust were going everywhere.

It was the wrong thing to do at that moment, because Mr. Demontavio, the owner of the station, had efforted his considerable bulk up the stairs and had just entered the room as Emeril sacked Ramon.

Good grief, my life as I knew it, was now officially over, concluded. The end.

23 – *No More Favors, Joe (S-H-Mouse)*

Mr. Demontavio had been known to smoke the occasional golden leaf and Fat Baby supplied him, and he told Fat that it was for medicinal purposes and that it toned down the pain of his arthritis. So I guess that's the reason he didn't clean house right then and there.

But the coke and pills all over the floor was another matter, and Mr. Demontavio pointed at the door and told us not to come back. Thank God, nobody called the cops, because if they did, we'd all be on the way to an orange suit fitting.

I started the car and pulled out into traffic and stayed silent until I had to have my question answered. "Why did you have to go after Havenetta?"

"I didn't." Ramon let out what sounded like an impatient breath. "The chick used to work for me when I pimped."

"She's a hooker?"

"She *was* a hooker, a good one. When she quit, I gave her one last woody and sent her out in the world. She loves me, and she has the cutest little beauty spot you ever seen and buckets the size of grapefruits."

Now, normally I would have been paying close attention to descriptions like that but they were just words at this particular time, because I had to start cleaning up things.

"Ramon, you got their thirty grand. Gimme a break."

"Why should I? There's no tellin' how much shit I left on the floor. I unloaded more than their delivery when I got hot."

"It's not my fault, Ramon. I didn't start the fight." I slowed down my word output. "In fact, this is gonna cost me one of my biggest clients."

Ramon looked out the window for a few blocks, and I guess the good ol' Joe Oaks common sense soaked into him.

"Okay. You got it. We're square on the two grand, and I'll give you another thou because... just because. But I don't wanna see any more radio stations, and I'm not making no more special deliveries with you." He looked at me and squeezed his face into a frown. "Yer on yer own."

"Are you gonna give me a name, a reference so I can do a carry? I gotta make quick cash."

He hesitated and watched traffic for a long block, like he was planning a broadside.

"Yer a frickin' non-stop accident. I'll end up in the ass-end of a cell if I do more with you than a grand a pop." He looked across the bay at Star Island. "No more deals, no more favors. No, Joe."

I figured as much. We didn't talk for the rest of the ride.

I dumped Ramon at his corner, and when he got out of the Toyota he slammed the door without looking back with his usual reverse step victory signs.

24 – *You Gotta Love a Girl Like Katya*

I sat at the light, tapping the steering wheel and watching Ramon in my rearview mirror. He disappeared into the distance, probably along with my very necessary future merchandise, the dope, the plugola that I needed to buy airplay.

I turned my attention to the now-stuff to be handled. There was no point in calling Kodi. It was supposed to be a freebee anyway, and I had nothing to tell him. He'd probably already heard about the pileup in the studio, and if I got the airplay from Emeril and Fat it'd be a frickin' miracle, especially after being told by the station's owner not to come back.

The Naval Girl airplay disaster-count was now two for two, and I could probably write off Kodi's business as a result.

I was one day closer to the drop-deadline and sixty-three thousand bucks short, plus whatever Katya was charging at the hotel, which reminded me.

I fished out the cell phone and called her closet, which relayed me to her purse. Thank God I wasn't there to hear the first six notes *of I Could Have Danced All Night*, which is what she's got her cell set to play when she doesn't answer. I began to question my judgment for phoning, but hell, I needed to be stroked. She answered on the third ring.

"Joe, darling! I was just thinkin' about you!"

"Me, too."

"You were thinking about you? Not about me?"

"No, Katya, I was thinking about *you*." I felt like I was in one of those SNL scenes. "Say, can we get together?"

"After I finish getting my hair and nails done, and a pedicure. You know how you like my toes. I'm at the salon in the hotel. –Uh, Joe?"

"What?"

"I hope you don't mind, I'm charging it to my room. I'm a little short."

What the hell's the difference, sixty-three thousand or sixty-three thousand two hundred? "No, Katya, go ahead."

"Ooo-o, you're such a doll! I'll be ready at six! Gotta go, shampoo girl's ready for me." She clicked off.

You gotta love a girl like Katya, Catherine Lucille. All up front, in more ways than one.

At least tonight, alone with her, I could turn off the day and build some strength for figuring out how the hell I was going to crack the nut tomorrow.

But, what I needed was the nutcracker.

25 – *Early Returns & Blinky Eyes*

Katya was ready right on time.

But we had issues. She had just received a call from one Mr. Darragh Cahoone, and he was coming back a week sooner. And almost as bad, Katya was afraid to be alone with the fire-cleanup boys, one of which she said was eyeing her and winking a lot when doing the estimate.

"I want to be pure for you, from now on, Joe." Well, how could I refuse a girl with blinky eyes and a rack that that.

"Don't worry about it. I'll be there in the morning to get 'em started. Give me your key again."

"Oh, Joe, you're such a doll!" She stripped her condo key off her chain and handed it to me with dimples. I, of course, melted, again.

26 – A Lot of Incognito

I got there early, 7777 Collins Avenue, Penthouse Floor, Number A-1. Here, some yahoo was keeping a woman like Katya--okay, Catherine Lucille--and treating her like a sex slave.

What kind of little Camelot could I make for myself if I only had the big bucks? I know one thing, I'd make Catherine Lucille happy--make that Katya, I like that better--and I'd make myself a happy man in the process. *Why couldn't I get to the point of affording this whole scene,* I kept thinking as I keyed the lock and stepped inside the smoky condo.

I checked my watch. I had a half-hour before the cleaning guys were supposed to arrive, so I ran the tally and totaled up my assets. I had a few bucks to commit, and I could cover a bunch by maxing out my credit cards, but I'd still be short, and making a quick score with Ramon's contacts dimmed as a solution.

This guy Cahoone was some kind of importer all right, and I wondered again if Katya had any inkling that thirty million bucks, give or take, lurked behind the wall. If she did, she certainly wouldn't have been worried about where the money was coming from to pay for those fancy little seashell designs on her toenails.

Well, it was then that I had the urge to grab a box or two, seal up the rest and run like hell, never to be heard from again. A million-six would buy a lot of incognito.

But, I thought of Katya, and she said he'd kill her if he found out about all the damage and me, and all that went on between us. So, my conscience kicked in and I sat down in Cahoone's big leather chair to think.

I began to drift toward islands and I could see this picture of myself in cutoffs smiling and paying waitresses and bar tabs with hundred-dollar bills, all the time with Katya in a bikini looking up at me and laughing and leaning on my shoulder. I gotta admit that was pretty damned tempting.

The buzzing of the front door security system yanked me back into present jam reality. I half ran to the front door, answered the intercom and told the smoke damage cleanup guys to come on up. They did, and they drug in all manner of machines and cleaning gear and went to work, and I went back to Cahoone's office to sit on guard duty and do some dreaming. Nobody else was going to accidentally discover that mother lode like I did.

And then I began to think again, something I was doing a lot of the last few days. --I could take a couple of boxes, leave the crawlspace door open and take off. Anything that was missing could be blamed on the cleanup crew.

But again, the Katya issue came up. Like she said, he'd kill her and I couldn't risk that. She was too special in too many ways.

Back to square one.

A whole box would be missed. Hell, a stack, or two-thirds of a stack would be missed. But if I took two bills, two C-notes out of every hundred grand batch and carefully resealed each box, I'd have sixty-four thousand. Cahoone could not possibly notice them gone unless he counted it all, and even then he'd think the counting machine was off, or he'd assume whoever packaged up the cash pilfered a couple of bills from each stack. Could I get away with it?

Hell no, he's the one who probably counted it into the boxes, and he'd know it had been messed with.

Back to square one, again.

At the very least I could *borrow* the money and figure out a way to replace it as I earned paybacks from my music clients.

Throughout the day I drifted from island to island as Katya changed bikinis and I kept up the dispersal of C-notes into outstretched hands of widely smiling natives.

To hell with it. I shook off all my stupid thinking and lofty ideas. I made sure the cleanup guys were in the other end of the condo and I took the box I'd previously opened out from the crawl space and sat it on the edge of the desk. Then I sealed up the rest behind the wall just like nobody had ever shined the light of day on their little brown cardboard asses.

I could change my mind later.

27 – *One Fine Beaver*

I sat at Cahoone's big carved desk through lunch and all the way to five o'clock without anything except imaginary seafood and piña coladas hula-hula-ing through my head when Milagro, the lead cleanup guy, rapped on the door-facing.

"Time to go, señor. We come back tomorrow at nine to feenish up, hokay?" Milagro was the guy that put the eye on Katya and spooked her, and right now I was only tolerating him with about half my brain because most of my rapt attention was focused on King Solomon's mines, although what I was thinking could get me into a whole shit-pot full of trouble.

"I'll be right here waiting for you."

He flashed a smile by raising his left upper lip exposing a big gold tooth, the second one I'd seen this week. "Where's the señora of the house?"

"She's, uh, out of town."

"Are you her husbahnd?"

"Uh, yeah–uh, no. I'm a worker, just somebody to take care of business."

"Do you know her?"

"Uh, no." Lie, lie, lie. "Never met her. I just work on jobs like this." What a liar I'd learned how to be. Here I am balling her brains out and setting fire to her house and I can't even admit I know her. What a Judas.

"Well, you should get a look, señor. She is one fine beaver!"

That son-of-a-bitch, I wanted to leap up and punch his gold tooth out. He was now talking about my woman, but I had to keep my cool.

"Beaver, yeah."

"What?" he asked.

"I've seen it." I spoke before thinking, common for me lately.

"Huh?" Milagro looked a little puzzled.

"–I, uh, what time are you coming tomorrow, nine?"

"Yeah. Nine, señor."

"And you'll be finished by…

"Three."

"Good, goodbye." *Get the hell out before I lose my mind.* I'm sitting here guarding thirty million dollars and a woman that turns every head within oogle-distance and she isn't even here.

"We see you then, señor. And we require payment in full before we leave. Cashier's check."

"I'll pay in cash." Crap, I shouldn't have said that. His eyes lit up like the Jumbo Screen on Times Square.

"That's good, señor! That's good. Do you have it weeth you now?" Robbery time. *Joe Oaks found dead in lover's husband's study with a letter opener up his ass.*

"Hell no! I gotta go to the bank tomorrow, just before you finish, and the work better be great."

He changed his tune. "Yes, señor. It *weeill* be, I promise." He backed out of Cahoone's study, bowing like one of Prince Charles's manservants after serving a little who-who.

"See that it is," I barked.

When I heard the front door shut, I bounded out of the all-day chair, picked up the ten-by-twelve cardboard box that I had bravely left out from behind the concealing wall, and found a grocery bag in the kitchen. With loving care I placed the box deep down inside, hugged the bag tightly to my chest and headed for the Toyota presently parked in one of Mr. Darragh Cahoone's empty spaces.

I remembered on the way down in the elevator that Katya said he was in Colombia, so he was either laundering drug money or he was legit and he didn't like banks. Fat chance on the banks. It was drugs.

If I lived through this crap, it would be fricking worthy-of-being a supernatural, unearthly, blessed by the Pope, mind-blowing miracle.

28 – *New Zippers to Lower*

In the car, my first thought was of Katya.

No, hell, my first thought was of the eight hundred grand in my watchful care. The stupid bank closed at five, and I'd have to guard the cash with my life until morning when I could get a nice big safety deposit box. Nobody with a brain would leave four-fifths of a million bucks in a car or in a hotel room.

On the way to the hotel, I had to jog south a few blocks and gas up the Toyota. It was close to dry and it took almost forty-four dollars of go-juice. My wallet was dry, too, except for seventeen bucks, so I reached in the little brown box and helped myself to one of the many new crispy critters bearing Benny Franklin's picture. Why use a credit card when you've got cash? I set the box on the floorboard and locked the car up nice and tight, walked up and got in line at the cashier's window just a few yards away. The harried teenage attendant behind the glass looked around his cage, probably for his purple pen, but whatever it was he couldn't find it.

"Don't ya have anything smaller?" he yelled and I just shook my head.

He shoved my fifty-six dollars and change at me and yapped out, "Next!" to the guy behind.

I'd been buying gas here from the same kid at least twice a week, so you'd think I'd at least get a smile or a thank you.

I settled in behind the steering wheel and started back up Collins Avenue. I popped a Milk Dud and dialed Katya on her cell phone, or in her closet, and it rang her cell while I was enjoying my caramely little treat. She answered and said she was waiting for me in the Carousel and keeping Tylerfrank company. What a doll.

"Joe, darling, I miss you so much! When are you coming?"

Ooh-boy. I wanted to come back on that one, but I had to be the gentleman, and especially so since I was temporarily married to the little brown bag on the passenger seat. It was then that I remembered the answer to my immediate problem. There was a good size safe in the closet in my hotel room. I'd stash the cash there and meet Katya in the bar. "I miss you, too, doll. Is Tylerfrank being good to you?"

"He's getting me drunk on champagne cocktails and I want my Joey baby."

I knew by that admission that I better get my ass to the bar before dear Katya got so juiced that she started looking for new zippers to lower. Shithouse mouse, I was already exhausted from doing guard-duty all day, but I was absolutely sure I could still get it up for Miss Poland of 1996.

"I'll be there before Tylerfrank can refill your glass."

"I need something filled real soon, Joey baby-man."

"Watch the door. I'm walking through it any time now." My girl needed me.

"I'm watching–and, o-ooh, I'm getting so dizzy."
I hung up and mashed the accelerator.

29 – A Bird Dog Over a Pork Chop

Last night was a hot time. I thought I'd died and gone straight to heaven. Tylerfrank had given my phony Polish princess the right amount of glow and we ordered dinner in the room, which we barely touched. I was too busy getting *personally* touched and vice-versa. I had a hot score in the safe and a hotter score in the bed. If life could get any better than this I didn't know how.

Anyway, morning came and we woke up in each other's arms. I told you I had died and gone straight to heaven didn't I?

My wakeup call came with room service breakfast. Then, I had to convince Katya to go charge another new hairdo to which she showed her dimples and didn't have to be talked into it.

She left me with a kiss and a long hand-stroke all the way down my pants and I almost took her again. But I had to count out thirty-four grand, six hundred and some change and be on time at the condo. I'd hide the cash in the Toyota and hang around until the condo was finished. Then I'd fake going to the bank and come back and pay off Milagro and his boys.

+++

I guess cash made the difference, because they finished early and Milagro proudly showed me around at the great job they had done. The place looked just like it did before.

I called Milagro into the kitchen and counted out three hundred and forty-six crispy hundred-dollar bills while he alternately watched the stack grow and looked up at my face as I counted them out one by one. I swear he was salivating like a bird dog over a pork chop. Then I dug down deep in my pants for my dwindling wad and counted out two twenties and the final seven singles. We were square.

"Is this, uh–off the record, boss?"

"It's cash, isn't it?" I shrugged my shoulders and looked at him like he was a nine-year old.

"I work for you any time, boss!" He grinned wider and wider as he tried to fold the thick stack, but stopped, and with his right hand, slicked back his black hair, and then put half the bills in each pocket. I swear when he stashed the cash he was smiling even broader and his gold tooth had a brighter sparkle. That five-figure windfall would never make it to the company books, of that I was abso-frickin'-lutely certain. Money sure makes people happy.

I inspected the repair job on the den's door facing that the firemen busted, and it looked good, like nothing ever happened. Then I stuffed the hole behind the door lock's strike plate with part of a folded up Milk Dud box so I could push the door open or spring the lock with a credit card in case I needed back in before the big man came back to town.

Next, I had to get my ass across the causeway to the body shop and check on the cars. Maybe a little extra cash would produce similar results and get things back to normal faster so I could concentrate on finding more promo business and replace the money before one Darragh Cahoone discovered anything was missing.

First, I had to go to a hardware store and make an extra key to the condo so I could get my ass in and replace the cash when I got it together. That would be tricky, but with my close relationship with Miss Katya herself I would not have any trouble knowing when her fake husband was out of town.

Now, why did I take an entire box-load of hundreds? Besides having the uncontrollable urge, I'll tell you why. Cahoone might check a box and find it short a stack, but I honestly don't believe he'd count the boxes, especially with everything looking so nice and normal. And that's just the way I planned on making it from here on out. Nice and normal.

+++

With the condo's spare key on my ring, I left Ace Hardware and headed for Precisely the Best Body & Paint Shop west of downtown Miami.

Emilio walked me to the finish room and proudly showed off the Escalade and the Bentley, and I gotta say he and Carlos know their business. The two super cars looked showroom new, and parked between them was the sweetest little red Porsche convertible I ever saw and which I openly admired.

"That's señor Ramon's Porsche," Emilio said. "I'm buyin' it from heem with what you pay me, and he's getting a new wahn."

Partly with my dope-ola money, no doubt.

Well, that gave me a hot idea, and I had the dinero in the Toyota to back it up. I should've pulled this number on Milagro and the clean-up boys, but I was too anxious to get their asses out the building.

"Say Emilio, if I pay you cash, will that get me a big discount?"

"Ah, you beehn talking to señor Ramon. Cash money do talk to me!"

"How much?"

"Ten percent discount. Off the record, though, no records."

"Minus three thousand even."

"Hokay, you gotta deal."

And just like that, I saved myself three thousand bucks, three big ones, three Gs. I was beginning to like this high finance, I thought to my clever self as I headed for the Toyota and the little brown paper sack with twenty-eight thousand and some change in it. I took it all except three grand, and gave it to a smiling Emilio with instructions on where to deliver the like-new, formerly hopelessly wrecked Cahoone Bentley and the blue hairs' Cadillac Escalade. I was beginning to see light at the end of the tunnel, and I hoped it wasn't another train heading straight at me. *No,* I thought, *the worst is over.*

30 – Overheating Body Parts

I casually drove back toward the Beach and took a few deep breaths of salt air warmed by the late afternoon Florida sunshine.

Biscayne Bay looked better than I'd ever seen it, but I felt empty. Something was missing. Someone, I meant.

I needed my girl, and I called her closet knowing it would ring her cell, since she was still hanging around my ancient hotel and did not yet know the good news.

She answered in her coolest accent and transported me to Warsaw. I almost forgot what I wanted to say.

"The condo's finished. The car will be delivered tomorrow, and everything's back to normal. What d'ya think about all that, doll face?"

"Oh, Joe, you are the most precious man ever. How do you do so much so well?"

I wanted to say something cocky, like it comes naturally to a winner, but I still had a loose end, a big one, to tie up before I could start bragging about my unsurpassed expertise.

"Tell you what, tonight we celebrate. Where are you now?"

"Tylerfrank is feeding me little caviar snacks and chocolate martinis, and I'm waiting for you, just waiting for you, Joe baby."

"I'm just a mile away."

The celebration began in my head.

+++

And a fine celebration it was. We didn't wreck a car or set a building on fire. All we did was wreck ourselves on good booze; and, of course, we overheated a few body parts.

When I blinked awake, Katya was on her side looking at me with her dimples showing, and deep-the kind of smile on a woman that makes you want to reach over and take her. But the smile I thought was sweet was something else. She had something on her mind that she needed off.

"He called me yesterday."

"Who?"

"Darragh, of course. He said he was tired of traveling and that he was looking forward to spending a few weeks at home."

I wasn't prepared to discuss that one. So I just laid there until words formed. It took awhile.

"Joe--?"

"What do you want to do?" I asked.

"I dunno. This is all new for me." She rolled onto her back and stared at the ceiling. "I think maybe we play the game until we both maybe know what we want to do."

"He doesn't know anything, does he? What would *he* want to do anyway?"

"I'm talking about you and me, Joe. Until we know what *we* want to do. You and me."

And that's when the dead seriousness of this whole thing hit me.

31 – In a Family Way

The next morning I took Katya on a tour of her newly refurbed condominium and she let out ooos and ahhs at the fresh, clean, new look. The repaired Bentley was delivered while we were there and she just smiled and shook her head and kissed me several times on the cheek. I gotta admit, I'm a softie for that kind of… well, you know.

"I'm gonna sell you as my cousin."

"What?" I had no idea what Katya was talking about.

"To Darragh, I'll tell him you're my cousin so you can be around, until we make up our minds what we're going to do."

"Your cousin, from Poland? You gotta be kidding, I'm not a good actor."

"Oh, for cripes sake, he knows I'm from Detroit."

"So I can be Joe Oaks from Detroit, your mother's older sister's kid, or something like that."

"Yeah, something like that."

"And that way we won't have to sneak around."

"Yeah, and we'll all have dinner this week."

I hated the plan. It gave me a sinking feeling. It just didn't feel right.

32 – Does It Smell Smoky in Here?

"So, Joe, what do ya do in Detroit?" Darragh Cahoone, a bulky man that reminded me of a New Jersey politician, put his knife and fork down on his cleaned off plate and leaned back in the chair at the head of the table. We'd just eaten a large chunk out of a catered stuffed goose. A cooked goose, yeah, I was thinking about the humor in that and how if I don't give just the right answers I could end up a dead duck.

"S'cuse me," Katya scooted her chair back. "I'll get our desserts. We're having triple chocolate fudge brownies." It was a bad time for Katya to leave. She needed to hear everything to keep her stories straight.

"What the hell other kind of brownies are there? They're all chocolate fudge." Cahoone leaned toward me, "Women over-explain everything."

Not a nice guy, I thought, even if Katya was out of earshot; but that was one of the things I was afraid of, she might over-explain me and get us both in deep doody. Like I said, there are no easy answers.

"So, Joe, what do ya do in Motor City, huh?"

"Oh, sorry. It's hardly Motor City anymore. I'm not there, I'm here now."

"Yeah, I can see that. You're sittin' right here in front of me. What am I, blind? So, what d'ya do?"

"Uh, record promotion."

"You mean like phonograph records?"

I nodded. "Yeah, CDs now. Some of us older guys still call 'em records."

"I thought the kids now downloaded all that garbage."

"They do, but they gotta know what they want to download and my job is get the songs known–heard on radio stations so the little fu… uh, so the young people *want* to download 'em."

"You're like an advance man, a promoter." Katya returned as he said that and daintily set down the three desserts.

"I'll bring the coffee, go ahead, don't wait on me." She left again.

"Yeah, I'm a promo man, that's what they call me."

"Hey, does it smell smoky in here to you?"

Oh, God help me. "Naw, it smells normal. It's probably just the cooked goose, or the goose cooking."

"It was catered, pal," Darragh Cahoone belched. "You know, I could use a good promo man."

Shithouse mouse. Here we go again. I smiled, waiting for the next surprise.

"Hey, honestly, Cousin Joe, doesn't this place smell like smoke?"

33 – *Future Dismemberment & Gooey Death*

I could hardly refuse to take the job, especially since I was now trusted Cousin Joe, and especially since my entire promo world had blown up with Kodi Graws and the rest of my worldly contacts–and more especially, since I needed to be closer to the knowledge of the when and where of my likely forthcoming future dismemberment and gooey death at the hands of one Darragh Cahoone.

I still had faith… well, some. But, I gotta admit, since I learned what I was going to be promoting, my faith was stumbling around on the rocks down by the riverfront.

"Drugs, Joe, drugs. Everybody uses 'em. Few people promote 'em and sell 'em. I need a good promo man, and if you're good at promotion of that jackfruit called music, rap, whatever, that nobody with more than half a brain really likes, then you gotta be great at promoting what everybody wants and uses. Am I right or what?"

Oh baby, oh baby, oh baby, what's going down. "Right, Darragh." Here I sit, already on a first name basis with a big time drug importer *and* in the hole to him for a foot-long box of hundreds, not to mention the sure death sentence for doing Katya.

Keep listening, keep agreeing, stay alive. "What do you like to push the most?" I asked attentively.

"Whaddya mean, push? We're not *pushers*. We promote legitimate imported drugs to legitimate businessmen. Gotta watch how we say things in this market!"

Well, learning that little tidbit was the relief of reliefs. I might even be able to actually go to sleep tonight instead of staring at the ceiling wondering how much time I have left on my life clock. No, hell, I'd still lie there wondering what Katya was doing in bed with Cahoone.

+++

I left Katya's smoky-smelling condo and turned my cell phone back on as soon as I got in the Toyota. There was a call from none other than Ramon himself. He said it was a Capital E emergency, and to call him back no matter what time it was. That's weird because Ramon had never called me before. I'd called him plenty of times, but this was the first from him to me.

"Ever since you hustled me for credit, I knew you were gonna be trouble, Joe. But now, you got a major, major problem. You're holding a two-seven pal, and I've got a pair of aces on you. Your ass is grass unless you fix this and make it right, and I mean right now."

"Ramon, I have no idea what you are talking about."

"Well, let me spell it out for you real slow, *bisnero*." Ramon was talking bitingly serious and clipped like James Cagney in those old black and white late night gangster movies. "I'm out a cherry little red Porsche, and I'm sitting here with $30,000 cash of which twenty-five grand is money that Emilio says he got from you, Joe. It's *funny money*. Whaddya think about that, Joe Oaks."

"Funny money? Funny money?"

"Counterfeit, Joe. Counterfeit. Don't tell me you didn't know."

I had to take an abnormal pause on that one, and finally got up enough wind. "I borrowed it. Yeah, it's borrowed."

"Nobody loans counterfeit C-notes, Joe. They'd be locked up for fucking life."

"--I didn't quite borrow them. I sort of took 'em on loan."

Ramon took the longest pause of the call. "You stole 'em, didn't you, Joe?"

"No, I--borrowed--"

"You stole 'em. I knew it, damn it! And your problem is now my problem."

34 – Sweet-talkin' Sugarcoated Candyman

So, we're sitting in Denny's and I couldn't tell Ramon that I was shagging Katya; that would complicate matters way too much. I just told him about being her cousin, and about her husband Darragh Cahoone hiring me to be a promo man for his pharmaceutical imports. Ramon listened, but after I said Darragh Cahoone's name, he just dropped his head to the table and banged it lightly up and down. Bang. Bang. Bang.

Ramon just kept banging his head on the tabletop at Denny's, not hard mind you, just hard enough to irritate the truck driver type guy in the booth behind him. He just kept banging his head, over and over and over and over again.

"Hey, lighten up on yourself," I said.

"I can't. My life's done and so's yours. I just didn't want it to be this soon. I can't believe it, I can't believe it, I can't believe it. I can't–"

"Stop banging. What're you saying? Tell me, my heart's starting to go too fast."

"Take a deep breath, Joe."

I did.

Ramon sat up straight and leaned in across the table. "Darragh Cahoone is the biggest Barnes Man in the country," he said low and slow. "He brings in tankers full of shit, pallets of pot, coke by the truckload. He's the guy at the top; my supplier gets his stuff from Cahoone."

All I could do was shake my head slowly from side to side in a near state of disbelief.

"You wanted to get hooked up, didn't you, Joe baby. You are now a family man."

"I'm… not, I'm–oh, Mother Mary Martin."

"But that's not the worst of it. He's also a beat artist."

"What? A who?"

"A real pill zoomer, he sells fake real drugs all over the fuckin' planet Earth. You wanna know why the little blue pill didn't make your dobber go boink? Answer, candyman Darragh Cahoone."

"People can complain to the feds, or to the cops."

"What're you gonna do, run to the police and say I didn't get a hard-on from my illegally purchased medication? I don't think so. What's he gonna pay you?"

"Plenty, plus I get a percentage of sales. I'll pay you back from my first few checks, I promise. Please tell Emilio that everything's okay and the money's good, so he won't be talking to the wrong people. Will you do that for me, Ramon?"

"It's guaran-ass-teed Emilio doesn't know, 'cause he knows I'd frickin' kill him if he paid me in phony cash."

I was beginning to feel like Ramon was my only link to reality. He kept talking.

"The only way I can get even is for you to work it from the inside, and I *will* get even. Have you put any more of this shit out?" He was talking about the funny money.

I told him about Milagro and the clean-up crew, but for some reason I couldn't tell him about the little brown box containing the remaining fake $740,000 in my hotel room safe.

35 – Gimme the Jersey 'Wha'?

So here's the jumbo burning question as I start my first day of work for Mr. Darragh Cahoone. Am I selling phony name brand drugs, or God forbid, real illegal drugs, or what? I know two things, I am scared, and I am promoting drugs; but I don't know which kind, and I hope Mr. Darragh Cahoone doesn't get in the mood to count little brown boxes resting in short stacks behind the paneled wall that my eyes seem to be fixed on as I sit restlessly on the guest side of his desk.

"Joe, Joe, Joe. I'm so glad you accepted my little offer. If you can sell that crap kid music, you can certainly, we'll say, 'promote' what most ev'rybody wants. Your big job will be to get the word out, to the right people of course, of who's got the good stuff."

"I think I understand, Mr. Cahoone."

"It's Darragh to you, Joe boy; you're family– and, you know I travel a lot– so since you're family, I want you to personally keep a watch over my little girl and take real good care of her, as I know you will."

The thought occurred to me, yeah, I take real good care of her now, and you'd kill me if you knew how good.

"I'll be happy to do that, uh, Darragh. Happy." I nodded, with the resolve of a real ethical son-of-a-bitch. Good grief, the dike is bursting and I'm standing under it.

"And, you're gonna love this next part. If you do real good on selling my exclusive line to a *select* group of pharmacists and mail order gurus, you get to advance to the big time and travel to some pretty exotic places, a lot better than good ol' Miami Beach here. Do you like that?"

"Sounds good to–"

"Now, as I explain things to you, you're gonna get that this is a kinda high risk business, so I pay real well for you to follow instructions real well, get it?"

"Yes sir."

"Sir? Hell, man, I'm just your cousin-in-law, not your daddy. Just nod if you understand, and gimme the Jersey 'Wha?' if you don't, okay?"

I nodded. Cahoone became more Hoboken by the second.

"So here's the deal, I give you a thousand a day, five grand a week, against ten-percent of all the brand names and designers you sell. You take two days off a week to learn how to spend all that cash, okay? Isn't that better than pushin' rap music to radio stations?"

I nodded. For a thousand a day, I'd sell Communion wafers to starving Catholics--or maybe not. I'm not quite that money-grubbing. The thought occurred to me though, that a thousand a day would rack up in a hurry, and I could replace that little box behind the panel wall with it's full complement of eight-hundred grand inside, and I could do that real soon.

But, and it was a mighty big but, I'd be putting sixty grand of real money in the box to replace phony money. That didn't make sense. I had to think that one out.

Cahoone yammered on and I was listening, but I was also thinking about my doll still asleep in the Master Suite, and I was wondering when Mr. Darragh Cahoone was going to take another flight out of town.

"I'll be leaving The Beach in about a week, Joe, just as soon as you understand what to do and how to do it. Now, do ya need any cash to get started? A little advance money, cousin?"

Now that little reveal floored me, but I had to look like I was thinking it out even though I knew the answer immediately.

I paused, looked down and from my inside coat pocket, pulled out my wallet and looked at my checkbook therein, and finally said like a big-time hood dealer, "Oh, about thirty large will take care of me."

Cahoone leaned back and took a long beat. "What are you, starting your own casino? Shit, man, I'm only gonna be gone for two weeks. I'll give you ten. At least I know you think big."

Hey, I had to take the shot. I leaned forward and stuck out my hand and said in my most sincere businesslike manner, "Thanks, Darragh, that'll be enough to keep me going 'til you get back."

"Criminies, I should hope so. You fricking guys in the music business must make out pretty good." He tapped a Marlboro out of the package and lit up. "That five large a week includes expenses, so take my girl out for a couple of dinners. Okay, cousin? Watch out for her and don't let her get in trouble. When she has a couple o' drinks, she gets a little frisky, but you, being her cousin and all, probably know she likes to have a good time."

I nodded and fixed my mouth like I knew exactly what he meant; and boy, did I ever know, first hand, up close and personal. Yabba dabba do.

He took a long drag on the Marlboro and coughed.

"Now, let's talk about the nitty-gritty, how you earn your upkeep, and what I expect you to have done by the time I get back..."

36 – Crapola, I've Got a Partner

Ramon waited at his usual South Beach corner. The object of my meeting was to talk him into helping me communicate with open-minded Cuban pharmacy owners on backroom ways to increase their profit margins, and Cuban club owners who like to have a few high-markup recreational pills and tabs on hand for their all-nighters and special customers.

I paralleled the curb and he hopped in.

"I get half."

Well, crapola, just like that I had a partner, not exactly what I had in mind. I pulled out into traffic and let a few blocks pass before I opened my big mouth.

"Yeah, I'll get you paid back, then we renegotiate."

"Okay, *ñaño*. We just renegotiated in advance. I get half, Mr. Negotiator."

He had me by the nuts. Overall, not a bad deal. I get to keep my arms, head, legs, and fingers, and Ramon gets paid back faster. Besides, if Ramon can open up doors in a speedy fashion, maybe both of us can score and get comfortable in the process.

"Okay, Ramon. You're on." You got to admit it when you have no bargaining power. "Now teach me some Cuban lingo."

+++

Sixteen. Precisely sixteen words and phrases to be exact. All I needed to know to double-team.

"That's all that's necessary," he said. "No point in giving you more to screw up and maybe getting us both locked up."

I replied with one of my newest learnings, *"Bueno, bien."* Good, okay.

I was to walk in ahead of Ramon, point and gesture to him to get up front and center, and he'd take it from there. I was the boss, the headman. Ramon was my point man, the mouth. My job was to look all serious, dead serious and emotionless. If Ramon made certain moves with his hands or head, I was to look down, or switch my eyes back and forth, all serious stuff, and say the predetermined word or phrase that matched his gesture. We practiced about a hundred times, until I was thirsty and ready to have Tylerfrank pour me a big one. More important, I was needing Katya, Catherine; hell, I dunno what to call her. I got to figure out her preference so I do what makes her happy.

Anyway, Darragh Cahoone took a flight to Mexico City this morning and will be gone at least a week. That's time enough to rev up my blazing relationship with my doll, Miss or Mrs. Katya Cahoone; oh man, Catherine Lucille… last name to be determined.

37 – Sleeping With Cousins, No-No!

Katya's surf 'n' turf lay on her fancy plate, barely touched.

I looked around Old Forge at the lizards and their trophy girlfriends. Nobody could hear us in our private little corner.

"I can't be sleepin' with my cousin," she said.

"But I'm a play-cousin, not a real cousin." I leaned over and kissed my play cousin doll on the forehead and a tear dripped down her cheek. Oh man, how I hate to see a pretty woman cry.

"If I don't treat you like a real cousin, I can't keep track," she said. "I'll make a mess out of everything and destroy whatever future we have." Katya knew her limitations. "And don't kiss me in public; cousins don't kiss unless they're both girls."

I flashed on lesbian cousins doing their thing, continuing on into an elaborate red and purple velvet bedroom, and then I snapped back to reality.

Future, she said. I hadn't really thought about the future--mine, ours or anybody else's. She had a point, though; but I had to put it out of my mind for now. Too much stuff was still on the table to be handled.

I changed the subject and we traded a little small talk, the subjects of which I would forget before I hit the sack tonight.

+++

I took my doll home in my new rented Mustang convertible and was careful to let the doorman see me leave, just in case he was chummy with one Mr. Darragh Cahoone.

I decided to stay clear of Tylerfrank and my usual haunts while I was on Cahoone's clock. Tylerfrank didn't need to know about my cousin scam either, so I purposefully kept Katya out of the lizard lounge at the Plage, merry-go-round and all, until some time into the future to-be-determined. And decisions like that also kept me from calling Katya whenever I had the urge, mainly 'cause Cahoone could be listening, checking up on what Katya was doing, or me for that matter, especially since he was footing me a grand a day for other, shall we say, *services,* in addition to watching over her.

After all, I'd promised Cahoone I'd take care of her.

38 – *Begging Like a Beagle*

Ramon picked up on the first ring and turned down flat my idea to stage a second story heist. I figured he had the history of knowing where people stashed money, and considering his sizable investment in my future, would be willing to accompany me.

"No way, José. Yer on yer own." Ramon wanted no part of me trying to recoup three hundred and forty-six phony Benjamins from Milagro, the fire clean-up guy. "Furthermore, I ain't going door-to-door pill pushing until you got that little item handled, comprender?" I said yes and agreed to keep Ramon out of the mix until that big fat loose end was tied up, if it could be tied up without me wearing an orange suit for the rest of my life.

"Yah, I understand," I said. "I figured you wouldn't want to touch it, so just in case I actually got a Plan B."

"Well, I hope yer Plan B is better than yer Plan A." Ramon clicked off without bothering to say goodbye.

No point in wasting time. I pulled out the scrap of paper with Milagro's number on it and punched it into my cell phone. Plan B, *Mr. Honesty,* was officially in operation.

+++

So I explained to a grossly suspicious Milagro, my made-up story of how I sold my car and was paid in phony cash, and I had no idea until I saw the buyer's photo on the news when he was caught for counterfeiting. Milagro bought the story, but for a price.

"You son of de beach, lucky for you I steel have all your play money."

Yesterday, Milagro had tried to buy a box of cigars with one of the hundreds, and his friend, who fortunately owns the cigar store, hit it with a purple pen and handed the Benjie back to him and said, 'Milagro, my friend, I know you would not knowingly try to give me a counterfeit hundred. Who gave it to you?'

"That about scared the *frijoles rojos* out of me," he said.

"What'd you say back? Please, I hope you didn't tell him it came from me." I'd have dropped to my knees and begged like a beagle if I thought it'd make a difference.

"Well, señor, lucky for you, I told heem I do not know where it came from; but I do know I have over three hundred of the little sons of de beaches and I *do* know that you are going to make theem good or I have freends who will beet the sheet out of you."

I met Milagro in person and convinced him that I was paying him out of my pocket because I was the one who caused the fire, and not to bother the Cahoones since they knew nothing about the bad money.

I told him I had a new job making big cash, and that I would replace the phony hundreds with real ones as soon as possible, and to show my good faith, I gave him fifty almost worn-out hundreds from my ten thousand dollar advance. He smiled about as broadly as anybody I'd ever seen.

"Now that you know I'm gonna be good for it, give me the three hundred and forty-six bad hundreds."

"Not a chance, señor. They are my ensurance policy. When you pay back all the owed plus twenty thousand, I geeve you your leetle phony bills back, all of theem."

"Twenty grand extra! That's robbery!"

"So? Sue me, señor!"

Well, shithouse mouse. In chess that's called checkmate. Milagro had me by my nuts and was twisting like Chubby Checker.

+++

I was so good at convincing Milagro of my solution, I went back to Ramon with my Joe Oaks skills finely honed. After all, I needed Ramon to help make the hot scores that would quickly get him, and Milagro, paid back pronto. He bought my act and we booked the rest of the week as a team with me playing straight man at pharmacies and with club owners in the seedy part of town.

39 – Benny from New Jersey

"Ver para creer." Seeing is believing, I told the club owner as I turned the big dealing over to my second-in-command.

"You can speak English. Benny here is from New Jersey," Ramon said in a half-disgusted tone. "So, Benny, how many drop-pops do you want? XTCs, flunitties, R's & T's, whatever; you name it. Minimum order, a thousand."

"Three thousand of each," Benny said from behind his cluttered desk. "What about some good stuff?" He picked at his teeth with somebody's business card while he was waiting on my response.

I shook my head no, "Later," I said. "Not now; let's get to know each other first." I felt like the true big time drug dealer. Ramon glanced over at me and squinted out his customary 'I don't approve' look. I figured we'd talk about that one later, and we did; but not before we collected eighteen grand cash and I popped the trunk of the Mustang and delivered the goods to Benny. Imagine that, I made almost two thousand of my advance back in one sales call. If we could do ten calls a day–

"Are you frickin' kidding, Joe Freak? What d'ya think we're doin', selling advertising to strip malls? Further, you get eight-hundred, I get one-thousand. Now you only owe me twenty-four grand even."

"I thought we were fifty-fifty."

"We are, after you pay me back."

"What about Milagro?"

"Work it out."

+++

I drove through Hialeah on the way to the next target before Ramon brought up my performance, which I thought was pretty darn good.

"Dumbass thing to say."

"What?"

"'Let's get to know each other first', real dumbass. You're selling drugs, not trolling for a date." Ramon had more than criticizing my acting on his mind. "Tell you what. If they want heavy-hittin' goods, I'll sell from my own stock and cut you in."

That little wrinkle certainly provided a way to do double-duty and cash-in big time, but my Joe Oaks common sense kicked in right away. "No, it might get back to Cahoone, and he might have us both snuffed."

Ramon just kept looking straight ahead with his knees propped up on my new Mustang dashboard. Eventually, he came around and applied his worldly approval.

"Yeah, you're right. Cahoone's gonna graduate you to the big time as soon as he knows you can sell the little shit."

I took a long lead before coming back on his last remark. "So, what we need to do is sell lots of little shit quick, right partner?" I asked in kind of a smartass way.

Ramon never looked at me. He just screwed up his mouth and gave me the two-fingered V-sign with his left hand. I kept on driving toward our next appointment, a big time mail-order prescription drug dealer, and all the time I was having a big chill run up my back while thinking about selling real dope to big time hustlers. I didn't know if I had the spine for that.

+++

"¿Cómo estás, amigo?" How are you, friend, I asked the mail order guru as I nodded to my partner to take over. I was getting pretty good with this Cuban lingo.

Ramon didn't miss a beat and before I knew it we were walking out of our newest customer's run-down office in Miami's west side with an order for ninety-four thousand geetus worth of fake name brands to be delivered in one week for cash on the barrelhead. Way to go. Less than ten more hits like that and I'd be even with the boys and ready to replace Darragh Cahoone's funny money behind the paneled wall, not to mention that I'd also be on the way to major big bucks, preparatory to the good life on Miami Beach.

Then I thought about my earlier chill at the idea of pushing drugs that could get me locked up for the rest of my life and I forced it out of my mind, replacing it with Katya and how sweet she was, and I got kind of an ache in my groin.

40 – Collecting "Bahd" Money

The next few days went like a Hummer on high test. I made… actually Ramon made the sales and I collected enough commission to pay him good money for the bad, and to pay back Milagro, including the twenty grand spiff he conned off me, minus the five grand I'd already paid him.

When I counted out all the real hundreds on the edge of Milagro's desk I guess I showed my sadness while looking at practically every penny I owned laying right there in front of me.

Milagro picked up a ten-grand stack and held it out. "Here, boss. Take thees back, you're a good man. You keep your word, señor." Then he pushed a manila envelop toward me. "All your bahd money's in there."

I didn't know what to say. Naturally I took the ten big ones, fist-bumped Milagro and he smiled until his big gold tooth showed like he'd just dropped a bundle into the collection plate at the barrio church. People sometimes do unexpected things, and I guess that includes both of us.

+++

Next, I had to get Cahoone's funny money back behind his paneled wall and not get caught. He was out of the country again, and I still had my duplicate key to the penthouse.

Besides, every time I gave Cahoone the week's payoff, he always asked "Are you sure that's all?" and that made me increasingly nervous. I was champing at the bit to finish this dumbass mistake once and for all.

I made sure Katya would be occupied getting her nails done and a new hairdo while I did the deed. I told her the visit to the Plage beauty salon was an all paid for-no-reason-at-all present from her cousin and she squealed, kissed me on the phone and said she wanted me to take her to dinner tonight.

Well, what do you think I said?

Hotcha, yeah!

41 – My Ass Into the Next Dimension

I took an inconspicuous seat with the lizards in the Plage lobby, nestled the freshly sealed brown box containing eight-hundred grand in phony Benjies securely in my lap, and watched Katya enter the front door and head toward the salon. She didn't see me 'cause she wasn't looking for me.

As soon as she was out of sight, I tucked the box under my arm and headed for 7777. I had exactly one hour to get in, replant the funny money in the exact place I found it, seal up everything nice and neat just like it was, and get back to the Plage before Katya came out from under the dryer.

Cahoone's doorman was signing for a resident's FedEx so I just breezed past him and he didn't look up. If the rest of this reverse heist went as smoothly, I'd be on my way back to the hotel in ten minutes or less.

+++

Nothing went right. For some dumb reason, the piece of folded up Milk Dud box was shoved so far into the strike plate hole that I almost couldn't jimmy the office door lock, and after fifteen minutes of screwing around with credit cards and case knives from Cahoone's kitchen, I got a thin plastic business card from my wallet to do the deed. Open sesame.

But before I looked inside, I had this chill up and down my backside that the big man himself would be sitting behind his desk, elbows on his chair arms, palms and fingers doing push-ups in front of his face, gaining muscle tone before he casually dropped his right hand into his middle drawer and drew up the 45 that would send my ass into the next dimension.

I slowly pushed the door open and peered into Cahoone's inner sanctum. Everything looked like it did the last time, except no Cahoone, and there was a small table with an ashtray on it in front of the panel concealing the crawlspace. I moved it aside and went to work.

The previously knocked out wall panel seemed to be tighter, but it caved under a little pressure and I picked up the box of hundreds, closed my eyes and pictured which stack I took it from just four weeks ago.

It's a damn good thing Cahoone didn't need to distribute his phony stash in the past month or there would have been a lot of questions, and fingers would have probably been pointing at me because I was the only... cousin around.

Sweat was popping out all across my forehead and I took out my handkerchief and wiped myself down while I counted the boxes just to make sure they were all still there. They tallied out and I picked up my little brown box and placed it exactly where it originally had been.

Too bad the boxes weren't stuffed with real C-notes, because if they had been I'd have grabbed three or four more, talked Katya into coming with me, and we'd be off with new names to some far away sunny beach.

Okay, dreams... so what.

When I backed out of the crawl space sweating big and all hunched over, Katya startled me upright and I let out one big yelp.

"What are you doin'?" she said in a soft but firm tone.

She was leaning against Cahoone's office door with her arms crossed and a serious look on her face that I'd never seen before. I must have turned whiter than an albino in a dungeon.

"I didn't get color; I just got a quick style so I got out early. What are you doin' in here, Joe?"

I didn't have an answer yet; I just looked at her with my mouth open and she kept staring at me with that same serious expression and her arms crossed over her rack.

"We need to talk," was all I could think of to say.

"We sure as hell do," she quickly replied.

"But not here," I said.

I quickly replaced the panel, moved the table back in front of it, and pried the piece of Milk Dud box out of the strike plate hole, gave Cahoone's office-den one last check, and closed the door behind Katya and me.

I had to take charge, and the only way out of a mess like this was the truth. "Get your purse, coat, whatever. We're going to dinner and we've got a lot of territory to cover."

"We sure as hell do," and her look didn't change from the last time she said it.

42 – *While Snapping at My Pastrami*

We didn't talk on the way to dinner. Katya sat rigid in the Mustang looking straight ahead with her pretty mouth painted pink and fixed firm. Every time I glanced over she hadn't changed. There was no doubt in my mind that I had no choice but to tell her everything.

I figured the little deli on Arthur Godfrey Road about five miles from the condo would be a good quiet place to have my come to Jesus moment with the new love of my life and I was right. When we walked in, the place was dead, a suitable location for the possible funeral of my love life.

I guided Katya to the backmost table, the furtherest spot away from where the waitresses and busboys gather and chat on slow nights. I sat her down, and took the chair where I could see anyone coming, and I opened the conversation.

"Well–"

"Well, what? This better be good, Joe Oaks."

"--Let's order first, and then I'll spill it all."

Studying the menu, getting the waitress, waiting for the food, all in silence, gave me time to put thoughts together, and when I finally began to lay out the sequence of events starting with the fire and my accidental discovery behind Darragh's wall and the reasons for my decisions, Katya didn't touch her matzo ball soup or corned beef sandwich while she sat back and listened with her arms still crossed.

I kept going, talking and snapping at my pastrami on rye, and by the time I hit how much I thought about her, how much she was on my mind, and how I loved her and wanted to protect her, her arms came uncrossed and she took a spoonful of soup without even looking at it.

Now, mind you, it was not my object to swoon her right there over her matzo balls, but it was happening. The part about me risking my whole life in federal prison by paying people with borrowed counterfeit money and by selling phony drugs just so I could balance the books and back out of my deal with Darragh... the part about me clearing the way to finding other income so I could talk her into leaving her present risky relationship... the part about me giving her everything she deserved and so much more... the part about me laying awake at night wishing she was by my side... if this woman was only a little bit in love with me before she caught me in Darragh's office, she was a whole lot in love with me now.

But it wasn't a one-way street. By the time I finished telling her everything, I had a bad case of cavernous, bottomless, tender and devoted deep affection, tugging at my external and internal body parts--it was love sickness. It hurt, and I was scared.

43 – *Fast Talking & Twitchy*

"So what do *we* do now?" Katya asked as her cell phone beeped an incoming message. She plucked the noisy phone from her purse and punched around on its keyboard while the word 'we' echoed around in my head, ricocheting off bits and pieces of recollections from the last few days' events--one long reverberation of 'we' as I tried to force my mind around the idea that it was now Joe and Katya and not just old lonesome Joe by himself.

"I guess--I guess *we*--make plans for the future," I finally said.

Katya got really nervous, fast-talking and twitchy-like. "Well, we better make plans pretty fast, Joe, because Darragh just texted me that he's flying in tonight, three days early."

I sat stunned for a few long seconds realizing the implications. I had to get her out of this restaurant and into the condo and we had to decide on how she'd handle Darragh; and how I would too, tomorrow. I flipped out a ten and a twenty to cover the check and we rocketed out of the deli.

I mashed the gas pedal and the Mustang roared all the way up Collins. Katya started crying part way there, and said she didn't want to go up to the penthouse, but I told her to cool it. I told her tomorrow was another day and we'd take it one day at a time. I used my old Joe Oaks smooth persuasion and she finally caved.

The plan was simple; everything nice and normal, and then Katya would do something that would make Darragh want to throw her out. She'd cry and pack and go to stay with her cousin Joe until she could get a job and get started financially again. Meanwhile, I'd restart my music promotion business and give Darragh the old 'so-long, it's been good to know ya.' I had planned to do that anyway. Easy, over, done, and out.

+++

I pulled into the 7777 parking garage and what should greet us in the formerly unoccupied parking space was the cobalt blue Bentley that Darragh had driven to the airport.

"Oh, Joe! I need time! I need time!"

"Do this–". A plan hatched in my agile and fertile brain, coming as I spoke it. "Call him from your cell to his cell. Tell him you got his message, and that you're out, and you want to pick up a hot dinner to have ready for him when he gets home. That'll give us time to think things out."

"Good idea." She dialed and he answered on first ring.

All I heard was her side of the conversation. She gave her pitch and stopped.

"Uh-huh. Un-huh." An overlong pause while she listened; then, "Un-huh, I'll call him– I'll find him, we'll be there." Katya punched the phone off and just looked at me.

"Shithouse mouse, what, what?"

123

"He sounded okay, calm; and he said he's already in town."

"We know that!"

"And he wants to see us both at ten o'clock."

"Why? Why tonight?" I felt the hot flush of blood rising in my face. A ten o'clock meeting made no sense. Something was wrong, and lots of things could be. I still had collections from the past few days' drug sales, a stash of cash in my hotel room safe, ready to deliver with my resignation, but...

"Did he say I should bring money?" I asked.

"He didn't mention it. He just said he wanted to have a family meeting, and he actually sounded sweeter than usual. We've got about an hour. I'm so confused."

It was Thursday night and I sure as hell wasn't going to work tomorrow, so I decided the best course of action was to settle up early by giving Darragh all but my cut of the week's sales so we wouldn't have to deal with it on Monday when I had planned to officially resign.

I left Katya in the lizard lounge with Tylerfrank while I retrieved the bag of cash from my room safe. Then we sat in the corner at the Carousel and chucked down a couple of drinks in between carefully laid plans. If he said this, then I'd say that. If he said that, then she'd say this. Katya acted like Nervous Norvus and could barely concentrate.

I was ready to begin our little charade, but we were not ready to face what came next.

44 – That's Why They Call It a Bentley (Premature Evacuation)

On the way up the elevator, Katya kept repeating, "Let's not do this, let's just leave now. I don't want to see him." I had to practically drag her into the condo.

The door to Darragh's office stood open with the light spilling a bright v-shaped shaft on the carpet as Katya and I advanced down the darkened hallway. Darragh obviously heard us coming.

"Come in, you're right on time." Darragh's voice sounded friendlier than usual. He stood up and smiled as I entered with Katya trailing behind, and he motioned us to take a seat in front of his desk.

I felt like I was sixteen and about to be interviewed for my first job, but Darragh turned his attention to Katya.

"Are you feeling okay?" he asked her.

Katya looked down, avoiding eye contact, while I hoisted a brown paper sack containing a tally sheet and the week's receipts, minus my percentage, to Darragh's desktop. I held out my right hand to shake, but Darragh ignored it. He glanced inside the bag, scrunched it up, and locked it in his side desk drawer. Then he looked up and his smile disappeared. Something was wrong.

"You like to drive expensive cars, Joe?"

"Well, yeah, but I like–"

"You wanna tell me what happened to my Bentley?" A little pause, and he looked away. "No, don't bother. I already know why it pulls to the side. It seems to have a bent frame."

I almost died right then and there.

Darragh tapped a cigarette out of a pack, lit it, and blew the first big puff of smoke up toward the ceiling, which reminded me of how smoky the condo was when the fire happened.

"Do you know what it costs to fix a bent frame on a Bentley, cousin? No, don't tell me; the Rolls dealer told me, so I already know." Darragh took in another deep draw and blew the big puff upward as he moved his gaze back toward me, and I thought about all that condo smoke again. "Now, I wonder how my Bentley got a bent frame? Care to tell me, cousin? No, don't; I already know." Darragh reached inside his top desk drawer and pulled out a DVD. "Do you know what this is, cousin? It's *not* a CD with frickin' teenage music crap on it; it's a little item from Channel 5 containing a news story about how my Bentley got its bent frame. Maybe that's why they call it a Bentley, huh?"

I had to laugh in a phony sort of way to match the kind of wry chuckle Darragh put in the pauses of his disastrous revelation.

"And," he continued, "this DVD has a mighty tasty shot of the little woman here displaying her nips and her electronically fuzzed-out beaver for all of South Florida to see." He tapped the ash off his cigarette and I bowed my head and avoided eye contact.

"Thank God for editors in the newsrooms, huh? Huh, pal? Otherwise, our wives and girlfriends might be showing their goodies to everyone on the planet."

Katya had begun to sniffle and let out little pieces of sobbing from her chair behind me and to my right. I stayed quiet with my eyes bugged open and my mouth partly agape; but Darragh continued…

"Now, let's talk about a fire, a great big fire in my penthouse here. Would you like to tell me all about that, Joe-boy? Or, how about you, Katya?"

I started to say something, I didn't know what, but Darragh held up both hands, palms up toward my face and kept talking.

"No, don't. I already know. Seems like the super here knows all about it too, since he had to explain it when he shoved the bill for cleaning the vestibule carpet in my face a few days ago. So, while staying here the last three days, shacked up at the Sheraton, my attorney pulled the police report on the fire and I learn about two nude people dancing all over the penthouse here, and being told to move out into the hallway while the fire boys knocked down the flames. Hmmm, I wonder who those two nude people were. Let me see now, I think they may be sitting right here in this office."

Katya let out a long slow loud moan. All I could do is stare straight ahead while I came completely unglued at my seams.

"Finally, and aren't you glad — *the piece of resistance*. Sorry, I don't do frickin' French, cousin." Darragh fired up another cig and stumped out the short one in the crystal ashtray. "Take a look at this, butthole, and you, too, butthole's mistress." That was the first heavy salvo at Katya and I stood up ready to unleash a punch in Cahoone's face.

"Sit down, Joe!" Katya screamed. "He knows all about us; just let him say it."

"Yeah, I'll say it! The truth is you're freakin' crazy, Joe Oaks. Now, let's see. You wreck my Bentley, you burn my house, you queer big deals, and you're dickin' my wife."

"I don't know what deals your talking about and she's not your wife."

"For your purposes she's my wife. So, you want to keep breathing?"

I shut up and listened.

"I counted the boxes, Joe, a week ago. There was one missing. You tell me why you should keep on breathing, because I don't frickin' know!"

Not what I wanted to hear. More complications than I could bear in one lifetime pressed into a small sliver of time with "The End" prominently displayed on my tombstone.

The truth, crap. I've been balling your play-wife every time you catch a plane; and, oh, by the way, I've also been driving your cars, spending your counterfeit money, and burning down your house, all bonuses for no additional charge! Yeah, right, the truth. I sat back down.

"What else do you have?" I practically whispered, resignedly knowing more was coming.

"Just this, asshole." Darragh pushed a button on a black remote, and his plasma TV came to life showing a wide angle of the room and his closed office door from the inside. It opened after a few seconds of scraping and punching noises, which I recognized as me trying to get in from the other side.

The door opens and there I am, the star in a secret movie, holding a small brown box and looking like a James Bond character. I went immediately to a panel on the wall, set the box down and... well, it was an entire replay of what I had done to replace the phony money, complete with Katya catching me in the act. The play was over and the curtain drawn. All that was left was the epilogue, which is what happened to the characters after the story concluded.

I didn't want to think about that.

"There's not a dollar missing." It was right then I remembered the hundred I took out for gas on the day I took the box, but I decided not to mention it. "I paid for all the repairs, everything, with the commission money I earned." I tried to sound all truthful and convincing.

"*Earned*, past tense. You won't be working for *me* anymore. Besides, you're not Katya's cousin. I checked you out."

I didn't have much starch left in me, but I managed to blurt out a small rebuke. "I was gonna quit Monday morning anyway."

"Quit? You don't get a chance to quit. You're fuckin' fired, Cuuuuz." Darragh made the last word sound like the sleaziest, slimiest word ever voiced on the planet. "Now both of you get your butts outta here; and, Katya, take only as much of your personal shit as you and Cuz here can carry. Anything left I'm sending to the dumpster. Get goin'! And don't think I can't have both of you snuffed in a milly-second, I can and I will if you give me any lip. Go, go, go!"

Cahoone let out a short burst of hot breath and looked out the window. I think he was genuinely hurt by having to send Katya away.

Katya doubled over in her chair with her forearms on her thighs and her face buried in her palms. She looked like she was crying on her knees.

"Straighten up! Get going!" Cahoone yelled. "Out, out, out!"

I pulled Katya up and she shook me off. "I can help myself," she said in a liquid sort of way, and with that she stood up straight and yanked at my lapel and coerced me quickly out of the office and into the hall. She had regained her composure.

"We'll take as many loads as we can to the hallway by the elevators, and then load the car," she blurted. I can't wait to get out of this place. It's been a prison."

Darragh's voice came booming from behind his desk. "What'd ya' say? What's that ya' say out there? I'm being a good guy letting you keep *your* stuff that *I* bought, but you want me to come throw you out now? Push me and I will!"

"Let's move fast or he'll do something we'll all regret," she said in a hush.

I got up my high-end nervous energy and put it to work. "Show me where your stuff is."

45 – Offloading & Bellman's Hernia

In less than ten minutes, we had all Katya's clothes, shoes, jewelry, makeup, and luggage all sitting by the elevator ready to be loaded for the trip down. I doubted the Mustang would carry all her personal stuff in one load, but we moved it to the front lobby and I paid the doorman to guard it while I brought the car up from downstairs. Then I hired an SUV cabby to load up while Katya and I loaded the Mustang. Within five minutes we were ready to go and I led the caravan down Collins on the short trip to The Plage.

Katya alternately cried and pleaded for me to find another hotel so we'd be safer, but I insisted we could do that in the morning. She was not happy with me.

I noticed Katya had two medium-sized suitcases that were heavy as hell, and she wouldn't let the cab driver take either one, and she insisted that they be in the back seat of the Mustang where she could see them. I thought they probably contained her phony jewelry and other irreplaceable valuables, but I was out of breath from all the action and didn't give the cases any more thought.

When we offloaded at The Plage, my efficiency suite looked like the back room at a clothing store. Dresses and pantsuits, fur coats and negligees hung on everything, and there was just enough space for a path between the front door and the bathroom.

Katya looked relieved that we'd gotten it all, but then she glanced around the room and panicked. "Where are my suitcases?" She struggled for breath.

"The bellman said they were too heavy to carry, and he'd put 'em on a cart and bring them up the freight elevator. I guess he's busy with check-ins."

"Oh, no, no, NO! We have to find them, we have to find them now." Katya's face had turned to gray concrete determination and she went sailing toward the front door just as the bellman knocked. I went ahead of Katya and snapped open the door.

"Sorry," the bellman said. "I had to take a couple to their rooms first. He struggled the two suitcases off the cart. "Gaaa, these things are heavy!"

I pulled off a twenty and pushed him toward the door before releasing my grip on the bill.

"Thanks for all the help getting this stuff up here."

"Looks like you'll be needing a bigger room, Mr. Oaks."

"Yeah, right. Goodnight." I was rude, but I didn't care. For the moment we were both safe with at least one wall between us and Mr. Darragh Cahoone.

I turned the deadbolt lock, slipped on the burglar chain, and faced my as-of-now legal live-in girlfriend who was busy relocking her suitcases after apparently unlocking them and taking a quick look inside at contents somewhat out of my view. Then, she flopped down face first on the king size bed.

"Okay Catherine Lucille Bobo, what's in the suitcases that gave our bellhop a hernia?" I sounded demanding, even to myself. "I want to know now why you panicked when they weren't here. Tell me."

With that simple command, she rolled over on the bed, looked at the ceiling for a few seconds, released a breath of resignation, stood up and walked over to where the suitcases were flat on the dresser. She let out a half-sob, half-moan, inserted her key, and popped one of them open.

No wonder they were heavy; they were loaded top to bottom, front to back, and side to side with C-notes. My little bit of experience with estimating cash in stacks of hundreds came in handy. There had to be at least seven, probably eight million dollars in the two cases, and it looked all used and worn, like the real thing.

I just stood there with my mouth open. "Where–"

"Don't make me talk now."

"Why'd you take it?" I asked.

"I couldn't help myself."

"But, just tell me what this–"

"I'm so tired, Joe. Let me explain it in the morning."

I couldn't come back on her. My goddess was rescuing both of us; or getting us both in deep dooky with Darragh Cahoone's felonious money in our possession. Her wish to talk in the morning was, at least, mostly okay with me, but not here.

We spent the balance of the night making multiple trips, loading and unloading the car at a little resort type motel in Pompano Beach, where we registered as Mr. and Mrs. Joe Olson from Daytona, only one hour after I'd checked out of the Plage as a single man. Good grief.

We fell asleep in each others' arms, half nude and completely exhausted with me recalling right out of the sleep-gate a tiny piece of trivia: 454 C-notes ($45,400) make a pound, and I spent the rest of the night dreaming about weighing suitcases on bathroom scales.

46 – *No Conundrum Here*

While I made a little wake-up coffee, Katya fired up one of her long brown cigarettes and gave a little single-digit feminine cough before she started explaining from her propped-up position in bed.

"Three mornings ago, before Darragh *supposedly* left town, a guy named Louie brought up two large brown suitcases. I overheard Louie tell him 'Same deal as last time, four to one, noon Tuesday at the warehouse.' Louie left and Darragh wrapped the suitcases with a ton of plastic tape and locked them in his clothes closet."

She drew in a little drag and coughed again.

"Well, I had this *need to know* come over me, so when Darragh supposedly left for the airport I went out and bought what looked like the same kind of tape. Then, I picked the lock on his closet door and got the tape off one of the suitcases. When I opened it, I just stood there for I don't know how long, looking at it like a crazy woman, and then it hit me. I knew what I had to do. I loaded all the money into my own suitcases, and wrapped the brown ones up with tape just like they were before. So, you see, Darragh thinks the money was delivered all safe and sound." She stirred powdered cream in her coffee.

"Baby, it was." I lit up a Camel and engaged my reasoning power. "And he'll know the money is missing the moment he lifts a suitcase and it's light as a balloon."

"Handled. I filled them both with a bunch of books I bought yesterday morning. I was gonna leave him, Joe. I was gonna pack up and move out before he got home, and he came back early. And I was gonna call you from where I was hiding."

"Well, same deal. When he opens a suitcase, he'll know we took the cash." I pulled in a longer than usual breath, and I wondered if she really would have called me.

This was no Chinese conundrum. Drug-dealer Cahoone was also in the counterfeiting business and he'd obviously made a big sale at the laundry; all his phony money behind his phony office wall for all the real money in Katya's suitcases––yeah, four to one, that was it. And last night, Cahoone obviously didn't check the suitcases or we'd be laying on cold slabs in the morgue.

"Won't he think Louie and his friends somehow made a switch and are stiffing him?" Katya rationalized.

"No, doll, he'll figure it out, and he'll know that we took the money out with your stuff, if not before. Right now, our lives are probably worth around thirty cents apiece, depending on what kind of frickin' bullets he uses."

Katya sighed and began lightly sobbing. She looked exhausted, totally drained. A few minutes later, I looked over and she was asleep again.

We were hours, minutes, or seconds from drawing our last breaths, or we had to change appearances and move around, or get the hell out of South Florida, fast.

47 – *Give a Little, Get a Little*

I laid in bed smoking, staring at the flaws in the ceiling, while I put together a preliminary checklist. Somebody had to take charge in this new family, and we needed a *go* plan.

Grand Cayman was beginning to look pretty good, probably the first place the hoods would look; so I decided the better place to hide was simply tooling around Florida for a few days like a couple of New York gawkers until we could see a full picture of what we were up against.

I eased out of bed, careful not to wake Sleeping Beauty, kissed her lightly on the forehead, slipped into yesterday's clothes, and left Katya a note that said I'd be back in less than an hour with real coffee and Egg McMuffins.

Katya's two suitcases remained low profile under a pile of clothes and I lingered for a moment on the way out, eyeballing the two moneybags for my own peace of mind. Then I pulled the motel door quietly shut, making sure the Do Not Disturb sign was on the knob.

First things first. I hit the main drag and purchased a couple of Hawaiian sport shirts, big sunglasses, and a New York Mets cap. Then I popped over to Walgreen's on North Federal Highway and bought blond hair dye, red hair dye, and a pair of scissors. Katya was not going to be happy, *and* she was gonna pitch a major bitch.

Final stop, McDonalds.

+++

"Poo on you Joe Oaks! Do you know how much time it takes to grow hair this long? About five years!" Katya, as I predicted, was throwing her hissy fit.

"Look, it's a one-time deal, and besides it'll grow back before you know it." I kept a cool head, as usual.

"You want me to cut off over four years and look like Buster Brown with red hair? No deal, no damn deal!"

"How about a compromise, cut it short, but keep it blond, and make it look youngish like the kids do. Do that and I'll go blond, too." Give a little, get a little--maybe.

She screwed up her mouth and looked away, at least giving my proposal some thought time. I reached for an Egg McMuffin.

"Gimme one of those," she said, and I could tell the wheels were turning, maybe in my direction.

+++

My phone beeped another message from Ramon, which I had no intention to answer, and that reminded me to call AT&T.

After changing both our cell phone numbers with no forwarding, I was watching Fox News and wondering how the blonde anchor packed all those good looking body parts into one tight green dress when the bathroom door flew open and Katya, nude to the world, announced her creation.

"TAH-DAAAAH!" She flailed her arms out to her sides, presentation style, and stood there with a big smile on her face.

Well, I gotta tell you, she looked hotter than a sharp stick at a weenie roast. Short blond hair with spikes, like the kids at the rock concerts. That hair-do was bound to draw attention to her mop instead of her face, and there was no way anyone would recognize the old Katya unless they slowly studied her ample features.

"I don't... I can't believe that's really you!" I said.

"We'll just have to be careful around cops, so you don't get arrested for being with an underage girl. Now, get your shirt off, Mr. Joe Oaks. You are about to become my hot blond boyfriend."

"No red spikes."

"No promises."

+++

Katya... she even did my chest hair, and I gotta admit, I felt pretty *hotcha* after the beauty treatment.

While she dressed and packed, the new blond Joe Oaks, donned in a new Hawaiian sport-shirt and sporting a new pair of Florida sunglasses, rented a neat little storage unit a couple miles down on South Dixie Highway. We hauled all our extra crap to it, and were tooling up I-95 by late-morning with the intention of heading to Disney World.

One thing for certain, we had to find a place to hide the money, and soon, because it was way below stupid to be traveling around happy-go-lucky with millions of hot bucks in suitcases--more like brain dead, or dying to be more accurate; but I'm not known as Joe Oaks, the Promo King for twiddling my digits.

We headed north and just past Boca Raton, that's when I sprung my big one. I already researched Florida law on my laptop back at the motel when Katya was in the shower. There was no waiting period and no blood test for non-residents.

"Let's get married."

She just turned and looked at me with her mouth open. It was a sizable pause and I could tell she was thinking long and hard.

48 – Footloose, Everybody Cut Footloose

"When we do it, get married that is, I want things to be normal, and not under a huge black cloud, like now," she said.

Katya was right. We had too many plates spinning and we had to keep them all in the air. We let a few miles pass with me staring at the road ahead and Katya staring out the passenger window.

"You got a driver's license?" she asked.

"Yeah, sure, of course."

"What state?" she asked in a soft thoughtful voice I'd not heard before.

"California. How about you?"

"Yeah, a Michigan license, why?"

"Because you didn't want to drive the Bentley, that's why."

"I don't like to drive, period. It's a man's job; but that's not the point. What's the name on your license?"

"My real name, Joseph Aaron Oaksley."

"That's good. That's really, really good."

"Why. Why is it so good?"

"You become Aaron Oaksley and I become Lucy Bobo." She had my full attention.

"And?"

"We rent safety deposit boxes at four banks, big enough to hold two million each."

My doll not only had the looks, she had the moxie.

+++

By five o'clock, we'd stashed eight million bucks in four banks between Delray Beach and West Palm, each safety deposit box with joint access by Lucille Bobo and/or Aaron Oaksley; the "and/or", according to Katya, in case something happened to one of us, and needless to say, we held back ten-thousand cash to blow on our Florida vacation, plus ninety-thousand for an emergency stash, which we hid in the lining of my luggage. We agreed not to go near the banks until we knew it was totally safe to do it.

"When we're not banking, I'll be Katya--and you'll still be my Joe Oaks, won't you, Joe baby?"

"Always, always. I'm yours, Katya."

We were now just a couple of people from out of town vacationing in the water-bound Sunshine State of Florida, and it looked like clear sailing ahead.

49 – Big Ass Stuff

My doll and I stayed in the best rooms at the best hotels, and hit every top restaurant north of Miami. We funned it up at Disney World, Epcot Center, Hollywood Studios, Universal Studios, SeaWorld, Silver Springs, and dozens of Florida's little side attractions. We paid for everything with cash and we had the time of our lives.

Two weeks later, along about noon on Friday, we decided to see the oldest city in America, St. Augustine, and we were making good time on I-95, but we needed a fill up. So, I signaled and pulled into an overpriced gas station, which we, as captives of the Interstate Highway System, were obliged to patronize.

"I'm so happy, Joe. I'm so happy." Katya said over and over to the point that I believed it.

And I was getting pretty happy myself as I yanked the steering wheel to the left and straightened out under the canopy covering a line of a half-dozen gas pumps. I took the first open position, leaving the last pump behind me ready for the next Interstate sucker to have his wallet deflated by the over-inflated prices. And here he came; or they, up close and personal right behind me.

It looked like the same dark blue Lincoln SUV that was parked next to us at the Ocala motel where we stayed last night. Shithouse mouse, that was way too much of a coincidence to be a coincidence.

I looked down as I exited the Mustang, went straight for the cashier and flipped him a couple of twenties. My dark sunglasses let me check out the man and woman inside and they couldn't see me eyeballing them. Strange though, both of them were looking straight at me, and at Katya, too, like we were sacks of Big Macs in a locker room full of football players.

The guy in the driver's seat opened the car door and unfolded, and he was a lot bigger than his face appeared through the SUV's windshield. The woman kept looking back and forth between Katya and me, like she was some sort of serious sentry commissioned to kill if her prey tried to get away. I felt a cold chill run up and down my back and neck and into the base of my brain. What the hell was going on here?

The big guy, two hundred pounds plus of muscle bulging a black t-shirt, came straight toward me, unsmiling, and he deliberately put his hand over my hand as I inserted the gas nozzle in the Mustang. I tilted my head up to face him with my mouth open, and he looked down at me except smiling now like he'd known me all his life.

"We're gonna get some big ass stuff handled, buddy-buddy, and you, minus your little girlfriend, are gonna chip in and help us get 'er done."

50 – Falling Down a Rabbit Hole

An eternity passed in my head before I could reason a comeback. It wasn't very good, but it was the best I could do under the weird circumstances.

"What are you talkin' about?" If this was about the money, my instant MO was play dumb from git-go. "Who *are* you?"

"I'm just a friendly DEA agent assigned to find out more about what you've been up to."

Oh crap, drugs. He let go of my hand and his smile faded as he took a step back and seemed to be looking for a reaction to dissect or read something into, so I continued to pump the gas and play it cool even though my mind was misfiring on all eight cylinders. I searched for just the right uninvolved-in-anything, good citizen comeback.

"I—I just don't know what you mean." I looked into the Mustang, and Katya had turned around to see who was talking and her eyes were as big as saucers.

"Well, let's just say we invest a little time and see if we have reasons to explain things to each other."

"Explain what? We're on vacation. Go away!"

The big guy towered over me by at least ten inches and shook his head slowly from side to side.

"Mr. Oaks, I don't think you have a choice in this matter. We got a positive ID on your rental car license plate and we *know* who you are. Let's just have a friendly little meeting. How about I join you for lunch, and perhaps we can answer each other's questions over a sandwich and iced tea while my associate keeps your girlfriend company."

"I need to see your ID," I said, like I knew what I was doing.

He reached in his back pocket and pulled out his wallet and flipped it open in one smooth motion to reveal an official looking card showing his picture and Drug Enforcement Agency credentials. Full head of dark hair, dark green eyes that could bore right through you. He was the same tan ruggedly handsome guy all right, Travis Macintyre, Diversion Investigator.

"What's a *Diversion* Investigator?" I felt like I was falling down a rabbit hole.

"Rogue pharmacies, Mr. Oaks, and their suppliers, that's who we focus on." He picked his words slowly like he was playing Scrabble for ten bucks a word. "Let me tell you right now, we know enough about your recent sales that if you talk freely it will go in your favor."

Did you ever have a feeling like brain freeze, and you weren't drinking a Slurpee? Well, I was having it, solid ice, barely able to speak while playing high stakes with cards being dealt by a mystery dealer named Travis. There didn't seem to be any alternative, so I said, "Where do you want to have lunch?"

"A nice little place not too far north from here. My associate, Ms. Mason, will drive your car and follow us so we can talk on the way." He motioned to the woman in the Lincoln Navigator and she nodded and started climbing out of the big SUV. "She's with the Secret Service, so be real nice, y'all understand?"

I nodded at the big guy, but didn't know why. Secret Service, shithouse mouse. What was next?

"I need to tell my girl it's okay." I didn't ask permission, I turned and went straight to the Mustang's driver's window and leaned in so I could almost whisper.

"These are federal agents and I don't think they know about you. You are Catherine Bobo, and you don't know anything. Okay?"

Katya showed a big-eyed open-mouthed look like she understood absolutely nothing, and with good reason.

"Play dumb! Got it?" I sounded agitated, but there was no other way. "We're all going to lunch, she's driving you in the Mustang and you're following me and the other agent." I pointed with my hitchhiker's thumb back toward the Lincoln.

A too long pause, and then she finally said, "I got it, okay."

I pulled out of the window and stood up straight just as the big brunette in the business suit who reminded me of the old movie star Jane Russell turned away from her brief chat with Macintyre.

"Key's in the ignition." I tried to sound relaxed and she looked a hole straight through me, opened the door and slid under the steering wheel. It looked like she held out her hand and offered Katya an introduction; and with that I went back to where handsome dingleberry was standing.

"Okay," I said, "let's go."

"You drive and I'll give directions."

"I've never driven a Navigator before."

"You never drove a right hand drive Bentley before either. This is easier."

Holy crap. I didn't say anything. I just opened the door and got into the driver's seat, wondering *how much more does this fed fuzz know.*

51 – Scoring Brownie Points

We pulled around my Mustang and exited the service area. The women followed behind us.

"Get back on I-95 northbound and get off at exit 284. We're going to a little restaurant in Flagler Beach called Finn's. They got a great seafood basket." Agent Macintyre relaxed back in his seat and laced his fingers behind his head like a guy would do if he was gonna watch a ballgame on TV. "We'll sit outside, away from other folks so we can talk in private."

After I made the exit, it was a little over two miles to the beach, and on the brief drive all he asked about was personal stuff. Did I have children, was I ever married, had I ever been in trouble with the government or police; and to all questions I gave a simple *no,* or *not really,* or *I never really thought about it* type answers. Maybe this not-so-accidental meeting wouldn't be so bad after all, or good ol' Travis was trying to make me feel comfortable and soften me up for the kill.

He also told me that the other agent's full name was Perri Mason, Perri with an "i" not a "y", and not to make a comment about it because it was a sensitive point with her and it wouldn't help my situation when she got around to asking her questions.

"About what?" I asked.

"She'll have to cover that," he said, and that answer made me quite a bit nervous. What could a Secret Service agent possibly want to know from me? I thought all they did was guard the President.

+++

We got an outside table in the far corner overlooking the beach and Perri Mason, Perri with an "i" not a "y", took Katya inside and sat where I could barely see them, which made me quite a bit more nervous than I already was.

A cute little waitress wearing a white tank top with a Finn's logo on it slapped the menus down, and the G-man ordered the seafood basket and iced tea, and I said I'd have the same.

"Let's just get right down to the old nitty gritty," Travis said. "Tell me about your job selling prescription drugs."

I took a few beats and thought about that particularly worded first salvo before answering. Whatever I said would be my word against Cahoone's if they nailed him, and I'd take bets right now that Cahoone wouldn't talk--about anything.

"I resigned. I quit when I heard a rumor that some of the drugs I was selling were not the real thing."

The tanned fed boy looked down, made his mouth into a flattish upside down U and nodded slowly.

"Good answer, Oaks. Too bad it's not true."

"What part?"

"You're kidding, of course. I'm not gonna tell you; that's for you to wiggle out of, bro."

The old Joe Oaks rationale wasn't dead yet. If he hadn't interviewed Cahoone, and I don't think he had, there was no way he could know I didn't resign, so I took the remaining path.

"Okay, I knew the drugs were probably phony early on, and my conscience wouldn't allow me to continue selling them."

"That answer I'll buy. Good job, Oaks. Let's go to question number two. The girl, who is she, where'd she come from?"

That one rocked me back. I had to cover what Katya might be saying, or cover what she might be covering up, and make it believable. Travis no doubt understood that I was mulling over possibilities, because he didn't say anything about me taking so much time to answer each question. My Joe Oaks common sense was wide-awake in this real life game of survival.

"I rescued her from the guy who supplied the phony drugs, my boss. He was practically holding her hostage, but she won't admit it."

"Why?"

I had to come back fast on that one, but I had the answer.

"Because she's scared of him." I don't know whether Travis believed that or not, because he didn't say anything; so, I amended, "Or she might make up something." Am I a genius or what?

Travis Macintyre asked a few more questions that didn't worry me much because my answers were close enough to the truth to be believable and not sink me deeper in the hot soup.

"Okay. Let's go on. Who'd you sell to?" he asked.

Brownie points. "I got a complete list. I'll provide you names, addresses, dates and amounts on all the drug stores, and Internet drug sites--on one condition."

"That you receive complete immunity from prosecution, right?"

"Yeah, I didn't know how to say it."

"I don't have the authority. I interview, that's all."

"Well, ask. And if you get me off the hook I'll tell you a lot more.

"Like what?"

"Make a telephone call."

"Hell, man. I'm running this show, you're not."

I stayed silent and Travis just looked at me until he finally took his elbows off the table and sat back in his chair and let out a loud exhale.

"Okay. You stay right here, where I can see you."

"And bring a piece of paper. I want it in writing."

Travis pushed away from the table and stood up, and under his breath just loud enough for me to hear, leaked out, "Asshole."

He fished his cell phone out of his pants as he turned toward the walkway where I couldn't hear him, and where he could keep an eye on me.

I searched around for Katya, and I caught her looking at me through the window. She was sitting at a small table across from the big brunette, and when the big woman wasn't looking I slipped her the okay sign where Travis couldn't see. Katya gave me a little nod. *We might live through this after all.*

Travis punched off the phone, disappeared for less than a minute and returned to the table. I guess he had the authority after all because he tossed a pair of identical forms at me that said in simple language that the department agreed not to prosecute if I provided all requested information with regard to... and there was a case number and some other scribbling and smaller print. Travis sat down, handed me a pen and pointed to a blank line.

"Sign both copies." I did, and he pulled one back and signed it and pushed it back at me.

"Okay, buddy. You got it."

I picked up the paper like it was a deed to the Trump Tower, carefully folded it, and put it my top shirt pocket right over my heart. The Joe Oaks creative know-how had come to the rescue. I wasn't only good for record promotion; I was good for legal crap, too.

"Well, start," he said.

"I don't have it with me. All my stuff is in storage."

"Dammit, where?"

52 – A Forgotten Factoid

The Travis and Perri team agreed to let Katya and me travel together for the drive south, which confirmed that Katya had said the right things, or they weren't interested in her in the first place, which means they didn't know how close she had been to the Cahoone action.

Four hours later, we were closing in on our little storage unit near Pompano Beach with the Lincoln Navigator containing the federal cavalry practically stuck to our butts. I guess good ol' Travis and Perri with an "i" Mason didn't want to take the chance that we'd try to run. That was no option anyway, and besides the famous Joe Oaks smart machine had come up with a plan. If my analysis was correct, the only person that would know we took the eight million simoleons would be one Darragh Cahoone, and he couldn't complain to anybody because it was no doubt criminal cash that paid for the 32 million in counterfeit hundreds, which he was obligated to deliver. Therefore, if we could help Travis Macintyre and his bosses put Cahoone in a federal pen, Katya and I would be free to enjoy the eight million unless Perri with an "i" Mason threw a big wrench into my now well-greased machinery.

"One more time, go over the part about the money," I said.

Katya rolled her eyes, "I'm tired, Joe, I'm really tired, and I've told you everything."

"Just once more, it's important."

"She asked 'where does Joe get his money' and I told her you were a record promotion man when I met you, and the record companies paid you to get their records played on radio stations. And then, I told her that Darragh met you and offered you a job selling his stuff, which I thought was prescription drugs, and you took the job. She asked if you were still employed and I said no and that I thought you quit or got fired, but I wasn't sure which."

"Perfect."

"Oh, and one more thing I forgot. She wanted to know where we got the money for this trip, and she asked to see the bills in my purse."

"Go over it again. And?"

"And she glanced at all of them and asked me, 'Don't you have any larger denominations, like fifties and hundreds?' I just shook my head no."

Right then a forgotten factoid popped up from the considerable Joe Oaks knowledge base. The Secret Service not only guarded the president, they also investigated counterfeiting, which sent another cold chill down my spine, one of the day's many.

The fire cleanup guy might have leaked to the wrong people, or--and that's when I remembered the phony hundred that I spent at the station where I always bought my gas. The little rude sales clerk must have found his purple pen and turned me in.

But why were Travis and Perri with an "i" working together. There was only one answer that made any sense; the common denominator, Darragh Cahoone, the king of South Florida's drugs *and* counterfeiting. Bingaringo!

I told Katya about the phony hundred, and how we should cover it if it came up.

53 – That's What I Call Acing...

All four of us were standing next to the storage unit after I retrieved the desired papers, and the old dude on duty at Store-It-Here wanted us to move our meeting somewhere else and he was getting quite a bit impatient. I slipped him a twenty for his trouble and said we'd be another five or ten minutes.

I handed Travis my tally sheets with names, dates, addresses, products, amounts bought, and cash received.

"Cahoone would kill me if he knew I had this."

You'd think I'd given Mr. DEA the map to the mother lode. He smiled and clucked and moved his head from side to side as he ran his finger down the considerable bonanza.

"What else you got?"

"Nothing else on paper, but I may think of some other stuff."

"I'll need your cell number and where you'll be staying; I may want to meet with you tomorrow."

I gave him the address of the motel in Pompano and wrote my phone number on the same paper.

Then, Perri Mason put in her request.

"I need to ask you a couple of questions, Mr. Oaks, before we wrap it up tonight." She motioned me to the Navigator and we sat down in the back seat.

I was more than jumpy, leaving Katya alone with Travis; but there was no choice.

Perri Mason launched off with her pen poised over her notepad and got right to the point. "Do you shop at a gas station on Arthur Godfrey Boulevard?" *Bingo again.*

"Yeah, several times a week. I buy my gas there."

"How do you pay?"

"Pay? Credit card... once or twice I've used cash."

"When was the last time you used cash?"

"Let me think." *Play the game, play the game.* "Well over a month ago. I remember exactly; the clerk was rude because I didn't have anything smaller than a hundred dollar bill."

"Did you have more than one of these bills?"

"No, just that one."

"Where exactly did you get that particular hundred dollar bill?"

"Let see, uh--Kat-uh, Catherine asked me to buy her a couple cartons of cigarettes and she gave me the hundred. I remember she said she was out of household money and she looked in Darragh Cahoone's desk drawer and found two stacks of hundred dollar bills, and she said she borrowed one. When I got gas, I'd already bought her cigarettes at another place, they were cheaper, and I used my own money instead of the hundred."

She glanced at her notes. "Mr. Oaks, I don't believe I have any further questions at this time."

"Anything I can do to help, Ms. Mason, and please call me Joe." *And that's what I call acing an interview.*

+++

After we said goodbye to our new friends, Katya seemed preoccupied and tired, so we phoned Red Lobster down in Lauderdale from the car and ordered takeout. We picked up two Shrimp Trios, hot biscuits, iced tea and a couple slices of key lime pie, and checked back into the Surf Side Motel.

I was drained from the day of intense grilling, but Katya was something more. She flopped down on the bed and looked blankly at the ceiling.

"What's up? What's the matter?"

"Darragh," she said.

"Yeah?"

"He can't go to anybody and complain about the money we took. They're gonna nail him, you know."

"Let's hope."

"He's gonna come after us before they shut him down."

"If he can find us."

"Oh, he'll find us, even if he's in prison. He's got friends in the business."

"Let's try to think positive," I reasoned.

"Darragh's gonna kill us, Joe."

54 – Face to Face, and Quick

The Florida sun kept its promise. After I laid awake most of the night, blue skies and the big ball of fire gave me some extra get-up-and-go, but the words, "Darragh's gonna kill us, Joe" stuck to the inside of my skull like a dumpling in a dry pot.

Katya's gloomy prediction made me rethink the past two weeks, and especially the last twenty-four hours. There was one sure way to keep her prophecy from coming true: get Darragh Cahoone locked up so tight that he'd never get out of the slammer or communicate with the outside world. The same went for his lieutenants, and that required a whole new chapter in the Joe Oaks' book of genius solutions.

For starters, I called Ramon. He picked up on the first ring.

"Where ya been, man? Two weeks! We coulda banked a fortune! I left ya several messages and then got disconnects."

"Forget it, Ramon, we're out of business."

"How come? Whaddya mean?"

"I'm under investigation by the feds."

Ramon took an abnormally long pause before coming up with one of his usual profound remarks.

"Fuck! What'd you say about me?"

Naturally, his first thought was self-preservation. "Nothing. You didn't come up yet."

"Whaddya mean, 'yet'?"

"I mean we better meet face to face, and quick."

+++

We agreed on joining up at noon at the Steak 'n Shake in Hallandale, and Ramon was last to get there.

"What's *she* doin' here?" The master of finesse said it right in front of my doll as he slipped in the other side of the booth. Katya just looked down and waited for me to intervene.

"She's okay, she's in this just as thick as you and me. This is Katya, and she's my lady."

Ramon looked Katya up and down like he didn't know whether he liked her or didn't. "You were the girl living with Cahoone, weren't ya?" He didn't wait for an answer. "You know you're playing with fire here, Joe, and this is no ordinary fire we're dealin' with."

"Katya's with me now and she knows everything." I had to take control so I could call the shots from here on out. "The DEA–" A young guy in Steak 'n Shake's black and white garb leaned over our table to take our orders and I barked it out. "Bring three Steakburgers, three fries and three Cokes."

"Hey!" Ramon said. "I might not want a burger."

I shook my head and the young waiter walked away while writing on his order pad.

"We don't have much time. Listen to me, Ramon. The DEA knows everything about our sales, what was sold, who to, and for how much."

"Not possible."

"Not only possible, but true. They got it all, and it's just a matter of time until somebody connects you to me, and then your ass is grass."

"If all that was true, you wouldn't be here; you'd be locked up tighter than a tick on a--" Ramon cocked his head and squinted at me.

"It's true, everything I said."

"You son-of-a-bitch. You told 'em, didn't you, *chivato*." I just looked at Ramon and we all went silent.

The guy brought our Steakburgers and other stuff, and we ate and didn't speak for another ten minutes.

Katya made a little small talk, but neither of us added to it. Then, I broke the silence.

"I had no choice; get immunity and then tell 'em, or be put away for a long long, time. But I *didn't* talk about you, and I believe you can get the same deal I did if *you* come forward and tell 'em about Darragh Cahoone and your middle man."

Katya opened her mouth and gestured like she was gonna say something, but must have changed her mind. Ramon looked like he wanted to kill me. I ignored it and kept talking.

"The feds know lots. All I did was confirm some of what they already know. When they start pulling in those phony prescription hawkers, your name is gonna come up, and that will lead to your other activities, and that will involve me again, and we'll both go to prison."

"You frickin' snitch."

"You probably would have done the same thing."

The couple behind Ramon heard his last burst and had started to pay attention, so I dropped a twenty on the check and got up with the intention of carrying on our little meeting outside. Katya followed and Ramon, looking aggravated, brought up the rear.

When we got to the Mustang I put the main pitch to him. "My plan is we both go together, get you immunity, and lay it all out, the whole street drugs pipeline."

"And after that, what would I frickin' do for a living, for money, flip hamburgers? You don't know what you're askin', Joe."

"They want the people at the top. We can deliver. They don't care about us. We'll get off," I hoped.

Ramon looked away and took a couple beats. "You fucked it up, long shot. "

"You need to decide now. They're contacting me again in the morning, and they may already know all about you. If you go to them before they come to you, you can probably get the same deal I got."

"Just one thing," Ramon snapped. He turned to me in a flash, drew back and hit me in the mouth with a bare fist.

I went down on my knees and Katya screamed and I reached up and tugged her jacket. "It's okay, it's okay. I had it coming." I spit out a mouthful of blood and Katya scratched around in her purse and dug out a little package of Kleenex and handed it to me.

"Thanks, baby." I swabbed at my face and looked at Ramon, who was looking down like he regretted letting it fly.

"Sorry, I couldn't help myself."

"Will you do it?" I asked simply through my rapidly swelling lips.

"I dunno–maybe, probably not." Ramon reached down, I clasped his hand and he pulled me up. "If I did and I'm not saying I will, how would I go about it? –Naw, forget it. I can't do it."

"I'll call you tonight." He didn't respond. There was still a chance.

55 – Is That a Threat?

For personal safety, Katya and I moved a few miles up the coast to a motel apartment in the Carriage House in Deerfield Beach and signed in as Mr. and Mrs. Aaron Oaksley from California. Following a late fast-food dinner, Katya got interested in some dumb television talent show and I phoned Ramon. After answering with a rude 'Yeah, Joe', he was quick to get to the subject of the afternoon meeting.

"What makes ya' think you could turn me? I am what I am, Joe Oaks. Your life will have to go on without my help, and right now your life isn't worth much."

"Is that a threat?" I asked. Katya turned off the TV and started listening to what I was saying.

"Not from me, but when I tell my supplier why I'm not truckin' product, he's gonna tell Cahoone and Cahoone's gonna come after you."

"They're gonna take Cahoone down anyway, and they may shut him down before he *can* come after me."

"You hope."

"Join me, Ramon. You don't really have a choice, and you know that's true."

The silence that followed was longer than any pause I ever experienced on the end of a phone line. I stayed quiet, but I could hear Ramon breathing. After a half-minute or maybe more, he spoke.

"Oh, I've got choices, but--" He sounded different, slower, beaten. "Yeah, Joe, you got yourself a partner, again."

It was my turn to take a long pause. "I'll do my best to make sure you made the right decision."

"I don't want to be a crime-fighter. I just want to get out of this with my skin."

"That makes two of us. I'll call you around noon tomorrow with a game plan." I punched off.

"Sounded like he gave you a yes," Katya said.

"Yeah, and now I gotta make sure I don't get us both in more trouble than we already are."

56 – *Locked Up for a Few Hundred*

A little early morning Florida rain slapped at the concrete outside and Katya was still sleeping, recouping from the night session of relief sex, which we both needed in order to wipe out the tension of the last couple of days. I shut the door to the bedroom and made coffee.

At 8:30 a.m. Travis Macintyre called on my cell and requested that I meet him at nine in his SUV on the Coral Square Mall parking lot. He said he had a few more questions, and he wanted me to do a narrative, as much as I could remember into a tape recorder. I said okay; and I told him that I might have more to offer, and that it might require giving someone else an agreement like mine.

I didn't know what Travis intended to accomplish, but my goal was to get Ramon immunity from prosecution so he could help in getting Darragh Cahoone locked up for a few hundred years. Travis asked about the nature of the info and I told him it was Florida street drugs. He said he'd bounce the proposition off his higher-ups.

I dressed, left Katya a note, grabbed some Mickey D's breakfast midway through the nine-mile drive, and on the last half, rehearsed my Ramon pitch with the windshield wipers slapping at the hot Florida rain.

When I rolled into the parking lot, I spotted the Lincoln Navigator in the far corner, away from the other parked cars that obviously belonged to the earlier arriving clerks and store managers, and I noticed that there was another guy in the front passenger seat of the Navigator, a big black dude who appeared even larger and bulkier than Mr. Macintyre himself.

I pulled into the space on the right and cut my engine. Travis motioned for me to get into the Navigator, which I did, and I helped myself to the seat behind Travis.

"Joe Oaks, meet Roosevelt Gunner. He's with DEA and his specialty is street drugs: pot, coke, meth, crack, you name it."

"Call me Rosy," said the big man, who looked like he could pick me up and break me in half.

I got right to the point. "A man I want to bring to you knows more about street drugs in Florida than anyone I know of, but he wants immunity before he opens his mouth."

Travis pointed to Gunner. "He's the man."

"I can't guarantee immunity, Mr. Oaks. This is more serious than Travis's specialty."

Not what I wanted to hear. I ignored Gunner's remark and plowed ahead. "My contact is ready to talk now. I don't know what he knows, but it'll be a lot deeper than the stuff I gave to Travis. He won't come forward unless he's got a no prosecution agreement; that much I know for sure, *and* he's a key link to Darragh Cahoone's business."

"We got Cahoone cornered on fake prescription drugs," Gunner said. "It's him, but mostly his middle tier distributors of recreationals we want; because after Cahoone's outta commission, the street druggers will simply find another coke and pot importer and be back in business in less than a week."

"My contact can fill in the blanks, I promise. The people you want are the people he was dealing with every day." I used past tense because I wanted Gunner to think Ramon had already stopped pushing. My last few words must've hit close to the bulls-eye, because Rosy Gunner turned almost completely around in his seat.

"How soon can I meet him?" I could swear the big man was practically salivating.

"Gimme a signed immunity agreement and he'll be available tonight or tomorrow, take your choice."

He didn't answer right away, but instead appeared to be considering alternatives.

Finally Rosy said, "Okay, he's got a deal. Hand me the briefcase on the floor behind you. What's his name?"

"Ramon, Ramon Rodriguez."

+++

I pulled up next to where Ramon's new Porsche was parked at the Hallandale McDonalds. He hopped out and into the passenger's side of the Mustang. I handed him two copies of the immunity agreement.

Ramon studied the forms. "So they already know who I am."

"Yeah, I had to tell 'em. They wouldn't hand it out with a blank for a name."

He gripped the forms like they might grow legs and try to get away.

"Sign one, keep the other." I pointed to the signature line. "And I'll call 'em for a place and time."

"This is crazy." Ramon slowly shook his head.

"We're doing the right thing."

"I got serious doubt, Joe-balls."

57 – Career Ending News Story

Early in the evening, Ramon called and said Rosy Gunner showed up at his apartment with another guy and a voice recorder. They made him sign the forms all over again so they was properly witnessed, and then Rosy interviewed him for about two hours.

"Who's the other guy? I asked. "What's he do?"

"Travis somebody--he asked questions about our phony drug sales and everything I know about Cahoone."

"Travis McIntyre?" This bugged me for some unknown reason, but I couldn't put my finger on why.

Ramon continued. "I answered all of Gunner's questions, including about Louie, my main contact; but when the other guy took over, he was more interested in the phony prescription drugs."

"Yeah, that's his department. Once I figured out that they probably know as much as I do, I decided I'd be done for if I didn't play it straight. I told him all I remembered. So we should be on the same page."

"They recorded everything, and something you oughta know, the big black guy was curious about the fight we had at the radio station where Havenetta works. Somebody up there ratted us out."

"Probably one of the people who came out of the offices to see what was going on," I reasoned.

"He seemed to know about it, so I spilled it. Fat Baby, Emeril Green, how it happened, the works; but I couldn't remember the rest of the names. That reminds me. Gunner said for you to call him tonight on his cell."

+++

I phoned Rosy and he told me to meet him in the sports bar a couple miles from his office in Weston. He said it would be a bad idea if certain people, meaning Cahoone I guess, saw me going into DEA headquarters. Thin chance, but best to be careful and safe.

Anyway, I parked right in front of the fancy Ale House surrounded by manicured shrubs and palm trees and found Rosy sitting all by himself as far away as he could get from the watching and cheering Gator basketball addicts.

I sort of lifted my right hand to shake, but he didn't seem to notice, and instead motioned to me and patted the tabletop. So, I helped myself to a seat directly across from him. The menus were already open.

"Are we eating?" I worried about my doll and it was her dinnertime.

"Anything you want. It's on me."

I decided on a shrimp salad so I'd have room for more with Katya later. Rosy settled on a Philly Cheese Steak, and that fit. A shapely blond in a wine shirt and shorts took our order, and that was the last of the social courtesy.

"Let's get right to the point, Oaks." He reached into his side pocket and retrieved a small, sleek silver voice recorder and laid it between us, which made me a little nervous. "This is just to help me remember. I got a few questions to ask about your friend Ramon."

I gave him one little nod and he picked up the recorder, told it the date, time and place, and then ordered me to state and spell my name, and give my permanent address, which I did, but I had to put in my two cents.

"Hey, this sounds awfully official and like it's gonna be more than just a few questions."

"SOP. Everybody gets the same drill."

I thought about the no prosecution form that I signed and I calmed down. It's a good thing ol' Joe has good inner control.

The blond in the tight shorts and tennis shoes brought our food and a couple of beers, and we ate in between the volleys of Q's and A's.

Rosy Gunner asked a hundred questions about my past dealings with Ramon, and especially about our hoo-ha ruckus in the radio station when Emeril Green flattened Ramon on Havenetta's desk. It hit Rosy funny and he was actually trying to hold in his laughing and doing a pretty good job of it, but went real serious when I told him how much shit Ramon unloaded on the desk and on the floor before Demontavio told us to get out. It was then Gunner unloaded a bombshell.

"You may have to testify about them."

"Who?!"

"The four we have in custody. You haven't seen the Herald today, have you? Got a good write up in the entertainment section."

"Who's in custody? What are their names?"

"Can't remember exactly; uh, Willie and his female partner, a guy by the name of Green; and, this one I do remember, Fat Baby Wiggles. How could I forget?"

"Damn, that's almost their whole air staff." I ratcheted through a range of emotions on this one, knowing that bit of news sealed the fate of my formerly illustrious career as a music promotion man, but I had to take a stand. "I can't testify against *them*. They're friends!"

He just looked at me while he thought a few seconds.

"You may not have to bother."

"Well, that gives me *some* relief."

"Good. Just be sure you stay around where I can reach you."

He asked a few more questions about getting airplay in exchange for happy weed spiffs and the like, and I was open, and for the most part honest when I thought he either knew it already or had pulled it out of Ramon, although Ramon didn't really know what I did with the drugs that I bought from him.

Rosy's question-engine ran out of gas and we quickly finished our food and beer, and I excused myself leaving more than half my salad on the plate. I told him I had to take my starving doll to dinner because she didn't have wheels.

58 – A Big Launch After Dinner

On the drive back to Deerfield Beach, I mulled over the meeting. Something bugged me and didn't make sense. Anyway, I shook it off and when I rolled up to the Carriage House, Katya was dressed to the hilt and ready for dinner.

"Oh Joe, let's go to Miami Beach, to a really good restaurant. I'm so tired of fast food and bars! All they have is chicken fingers and buffalo wings. Please, please?"

There's no refusing a girl like Katya. You bust your hump to give her whatever she wants and then some.

"Sure, but not in our old neighborhood. Okay, doll?"

"I know the perfect little place," she said.

+++

A little over a half-hour later, I avoided a valet and parked the Mustang one street west of the restaurant, but I still had an uneasy feeling in spite of being in Surfside, way north of The Plage and 7777.

Katya and I walked around the block and into a small Peruvian restaurant with a big reputation. I palmed a twenty-dollar bill to the headwaiter and asked for a place in the back. Not a problem.

He walked us to the rear of the eatery, stopped at a choice table, removed a reserved sign, and pulled out a chair for Katya, who started slipping out of her sable. The waiter grabbed the opportunity and offered to check it, but Katya declined.

"Just drape it over the back of my chair, please."

"Yes, ma'am, certainly."

I took the chair against the wall and to the left of Katya so I could have a three-sixty of the whole place. *Can't be too careful.*

Our assigned waiter appeared almost immediately with menus and water, and placed them in front of us with a kind of high-priced precision. Then he snapped up straight and asked if we'd like cocktails before dinner.

Katya requested a chocolate martini and I ordered my usual Kentucky medication with a 7-back. As soon as the waiter turned away, Katya excused herself for the ladies' room and left me alone to suck in the sights of this highly-rated and decorated-to-the-hilt food palace--and to think, something I hadn't had much time to do lately.

I got two feds from different departments grilling me about two different operations involving the same people. I got a high-level drug dealer's girlfriend and eight million dollars of his money in four different banks. How long until one of them finds out what I don't want them to know? How long can I go without making a mistake?

There were no snap answers, and I noticed my hand was shaking a little when I picked up my water.

Katya returned a couple of minutes later and got my mind off all the crap and onto the menu. We ordered and ate like two starved fools, and I polished off my last glass of Merlot along with the last bite of a too-big-for-ten people-to-eat chocolate something-or-other as the waiter brought the check. The tariff was a little north of eighty bucks, so I slipped a hundred into the leather folder, handed it to him and waived him off.

"Let's get out of here," I said. "I'm not comfortable being this close to Collins Avenue." I got up and pulled Katya's chair out like the gentleman I am; and as she stood up it looked like she dropped a few inches on one side and turned her ankle.

"Damn! I think I broke a heel." She reached down and pulled off her fancy right shoe, and sure enough the heel was broken about three-quarters of the way up. "Oh, I can't walk!"

"Just make it to the front door and I'll get the car."

"Thanks, Joe, baby. You're the best."

She took her other shoe off and walked barefoot to the front and parked herself just inside the entrance door while I retraced our steps toward where I parked two hours before.

As I turned the corner, I looked down a dark street and couldn't make out which car in the crowded block was my Mustang. Considering all the loose ends and the risky business I was into, I thought it best to use the tools I had to ensure a little safety. I pulled out my remote key and punched the lights on, and there sat my Mustang, looking all safe and normal about a half block away. But it was dark as an outhouse in the woods, and I didn't want to be fumbling my keys when I got in, so I hit the remote start button.

Good God almighty! The sky lit up like a Kennedy Space Center nighttime launch as an explosion sent my car in several different directions and taking a few other cars with it. Somebody was trying to kill me or kill us both. What remained of the Mustang turned into an instant ball of fire.

I stood there for what seemed like an hour, but was less than twenty seconds. Lights were coming on up and down the block and people were slowly coming out of their houses to find out what the hell happened.

The image of the whole neighborhood lighting up after the explosion shook me back to reality and I turned toward the restaurant.

The best thing to do now before the police came and started asking questions would be to call a cab, which I did--and by the time I got back, Katya and half the people from inside the eatery were outside on the sidewalk yapping.

Katya standing in her stocking feet and holding her shoes and purse, looked stunned, drained, frightened.

"Joe, Joe! You're okay! What was the loud bang? Where's the car?"

"We gotta get out of here." I looked down the street and spotted what looked like a cab turning the corner and heading in our direction. I pulled Katya with me toward the curb as it neared us, and by the time it came to a complete stop I'd shoved her inside and jumped in behind her. Rap noise from the driver's radio filled the cab.

"What's going on?" She seemed breathless.

"Later." I barked out the address of our Deerfield Beach motel and told the driver to take the Broad Causeway and Florida Turnpike. A few miles into the trip Katya continued to look at me with a kind of deer-in-the-headlights stare. She leaned toward me and whispered.

"Was it our car?"

"Obviously," I whispered back.

"What do you mean?"

"We're in a cab, aren't we?"

"Somebody must have followed us," Katya said.

"Could be anyone, even our federal friends, but my money's on your ex."

"I'm scared, Joe, really badly scared."

I glanced up to see if the driver appeared to be paying attention to anything except the noise coming out of his dashboard radio and he wasn't; but I put my finger across my lips and told Katya to kibosh the talk anyway until we got back to the motel. The first thing on my list when we found some privacy was to call Travis and Rosy, tell 'em what happened, and get their advice on what to do. Cahoone and his boys were trying to take us out.

After we got back to the motel, Katya doubled over crying and went out of control. Then and there I made several decisions. First, call the feds and sound 'em out. Second, dip into our ninety grand cash stash, call a small rental company and find a undistinguished late model car with out-of-state plates. Third, move to a new location, preferably further north. Fourth, get Katya out of town and in a safe place while I figured out our next move.

Tomorrow would be a busy day.

The clock on the nightstand was closing in on midnight, so I set it for 6:00 a.m. and stroked my girl's hair until she stopped crying and fell asleep.

The last thing she said was, "I'm really scared, Joe–really, really scared."

59 – *My Paradise Surprise*

After several hours of tossing and turning, I got up a half-hour early and turned off the alarm so it wouldn't wake Katya.

By 8:00 a.m. I located a rental with Kansas plates, a dark blue Ford something or other, and the agency was picking me up at nine to do the paperwork. I planned to rent it as Aaron Oaksley, use my old California address and pay cash for a month in advance.

I also made reservations at a little motel in Boynton Beach almost twenty miles north of Deerfield, and I made reservations for Katya in Nassau at Atlantis on Paradise Island beginning tonight for an indefinite stay. The best part, I decided to join her for the first three days.

The main thing I *hadn't* done is phone Travis and Rosy and tell 'em about last night, dreading what they knew or didn't know, and what I should say or not say, and whether I might end up behind bars for some as-of-now unknown reason.

Screw 'em. I decided to wait and contact 'em after my trip to Paradise Island with Katya, but I did let Ramon know that I was taking a little vacation for a couple of days.

A few minutes later my cell phone vibrated and the guy from the car rental agency said he was in front of the motel, so I woke Katya, told her to pack up for our relocation to our new motel up the coast, and that I'd be back in a half-hour with breakfast.

+++

While I smacked over my pancakes with sausage, and Katya picked over hers, I sprung my Paradise Island surprise. Strange, she didn't act excited in the least. Not even an "Oh, Joe!"

"Do you really think we can leave now?"

"If we ask enough people, someone will tell us no, so we do what we want to do and I'll tell 'em about last night when I get back. You stay in Nassau until we know it's safe for you to come home."

"I don't know, Joe, I just don't know if either of us are doing the right thing." Just what I needed, Katya's full support.

60 – Black Twenty-six Twice

We loaded up our stuff and checked into the out-of-the-way Sunny Motor Inn in Boynton Beach, and by the time we unloaded it was time to pack for the one o'clock flight from Ft. Lauderdale to Nassau. We were the last two to board before they slammed the door of the Airbus and blasted off for Paradise.

We were both so exhausted we slept all the way, from lift off to touch down, a whole fifty-five minutes.

+++

And paradise it was. Blue skies and green lights from get-go. We got there in plenty of time to don our bathing suits, me in my gray Speedo and Katya in her pink bikini. Whatta pair. Yeah, us too; but I was referring to Katya's ample rack, which was turning every head on Lagoon Beach–the men looking longingly and happy, and the women looking envious, and mad as hell at their boyfriends and mates.

We strutted around on the white sand, gawking at the beach lizards and downing our piña coladas until we were half loopy and dropped to the ground, falling asleep on our towels in the warm tropical sun. Two hours later, we shook off the snooze and sand and dressed for dinner.

I finished first and watched Katya put the finishing touches on her work of art, her ample body and face.

Here I am in Paradise with the woman of my fantasies, and living the life I dreamed about just a few weeks ago. Besides my little problem with the feds and Cahoone, which I planned to have under control in no time, I intended to make the most of the next two days and nights before I have to blast back to the Florida coast and take care of bees' wax.

I was disappointed when she finished working on herself. I mean I could have watched her primp all night, making an already perfect woman, more perfect still. Good God in heaven; I had fallen, and I had fallen hard at the feet of this Detroit goddess.

Then and there I made it a personal commitment privately to me, myself, and I, to show her the time of her life before I popped the big question. I mean how could she refuse in a place like this?

+++

On the way down in the elevator, we were alone and I turned and pulled Katya into me, smelling deeply her French perfume and all the mixed female fragrances that tagged along on this beautiful woman.

"Oh, Joe. It's almost like I miss you already."

"I'm not gone yet, doll, and you'll be here only as long as necessary." I moved to kiss her and she turned her head away.

"Don't. You'll mess up my lipstick and I'll have to go back upstairs and do it all over."

"No problem." But I had a little sinking feeling; she'd never refused a kiss before. Oh, well... first time for everything.

The Royal Tower elevator dinged and the door opened. We entered a new world.

+++

Forty-six hours in Paradise, and we did it all.

We snorkeled and *snubad* and ooo-ed at the fish, and struggled and laughed as we tried unsuccessfully to pedal a paddleboat; and we walked in a glass tunnel under the sharks and fed stingrays in waist-deep water.

Katya giggled as she chased me in the little waves hitting the beach, and we slept in the sun until we baked.

Whenever we got hungry we found a different restaurant and I sat across from her so I could see her face, and the more I looked at her, the deeper I fell.

On my last day, we stopped in the casino on the way to dinner. I gave Katya a hundred and told her to bet her favorite number on the roulette wheel. She dropped it on black twenty-six and the dealer exchanged the bill for a hundred-dollar chip and spun the ball.

It bounced and bounced and stopped on Katya's number. She went wild as they paid off thirty-five hundred dollars in chips. She kept three thousand and let five hundred ride, and damned if it didn't come in again winning her $17,500! I told her to spend every dime of it on herself while she waited on me to call her back to Florida.

+++

I reserved the quietest corner table at the Café Martinique and pre-ordered all Katya's favorite things from champagne and crab cakes to lobster tails; and topped it all off with a special order, their flaming chocolate volcano dessert. The waiter lit the brandy and it almost exploded, and he served it when the fire died down and slipped the little blue box with a red bow next to Katya's portion.

"What's this?" she asked as she picked it up.

"Something for you. Open it and see," I said matter of fact.

She looked at me with her mouth partially gaping, sort of a surprise look, and I'd say with a bit of suspicion while she slowly unwrapped it, all the time mostly keeping her eyes on me, I guess for clues.

I looked down and didn't give away the surprise as she tore away the last bit of paper and opened the flip-top ring box containing the results of my recent labor, my secret scrimping and squirreling away chunks of cash, along with pieces of my heart.

"Oh, Joe! It's beautiful, really beautiful!"

"Pass it to me." While still looking at the nearly two carat marquise diamond set in white gold, Katya handed it to me with her left hand, which I grasped and pulled toward me as I slipped the ring on her ring finger.

"Are you sure you want to do this?"

"I did it, didn't I?"

"I mean--you know what I mean, Joe."

I took a long beat and looked at her, memorizing her face and the moment and my feelings.

"--Katya, Catherine Lucille, will you marry me?"

She didn't answer right away. Just looked at me a long time, and then finally nodded her head and smiled. Then she added, "I'll say 'yes' when we get everything under control, Joe."

That hurt, but I acted my part. "I wouldn't have it any different," I said it like I meant it, but I wanted my girl.

61 – *Always Coming and Going*

We stayed up all night, saw a live show, gambled, watched the sunrise, and exhausted ourselves in pre-engagement bliss. After sleeping well into the afternoon, I got up, shaved, dressed, and packed for my early evening flight back to Fort Lauderdale to face the music and the grind.

Katya woke up when I was locking my suitcase. She stretched her little hairless arms out from under the covers and over her head. "Are you leaving now?"

"That's me, old Joe, always coming and going," I said with my rye chuckle, as is my humorous nature. I reluctantly took the few steps back to the bed, leaned down and scooped Katya up for one last hug and I almost cried. I didn't want to leave her alone, and I didn't want to go back to the Florida mess, but I had to do it.

"Baby, I'll call you as soon as it's safe to return."

"I'll be thinkin' about you, Joe."

I buried my face into her neck and shoulder and held her a moment, and lowered her back to the pillows. She seemed all depressed and passive but I had to leave to make the plane.

62 – *Good Ol' Joe, Minnow on a Hook*

As dusk turned to dark, the wheels of the Airbus touched down in Lauderdale and made a little skidding noise, and my feathers drooped. The feds and the dope-gangster problem was not something I wanted to jump back into after a long weekend of love and games and feeling sand between my toes.

As soon as the plane bumped to a stop and cut the engines, I grabbed my carry-on and fast-walked down the aisle so I'd be first off, way ahead of the lizards standing, and stretching and collecting their junk. About the time I got to the front, the tin can's door hissed open and I hustled down the loading arm and into the terminal. And guess who was leaning up against the rail nodding at me when I came through the archway? None other than one Mr. Roosevelt Gunner of the DEA. As soon as I reached parallel to him, he came off the rail and fell into step by my side.

"I was gonna call you as soon as I landed," I said.

"Yeah, right."

"No, really, I was! How'd you know I'd be on this flight?"

"You're flying a major carrier. Did you ever hear of DHS? All we got to do is put out your name and in a few seconds we know your entire itinerary. Relax, Joe, we even had somebody watching you in the Bahamas to make sure nobody attached a bomb to your ass."

"You know about the car?"

"About ten minutes after it blew. You should've called us. I told you to stay around, why didn't you?"

"I was hiding my girl in a safe place, so she wouldn't get hurt."

"I can't fault you that, or your ritzy weekend. But be glad you had a good time. It may be the last for awhile."

I panicked. "Whaddya mean? What's going on?"

"We have a few plans for you, and also for your friend, Ramon. Care to hear?"

"Yeah, I can hardly wait."

"You'll have to until we're private, besides I got to keep you safe since you're the key part of the plan."

"Oh, great, another reason to get me killed."

"You're not too far from wrong, bait."

"What'd you call me?"

"Bait."

+++

I could barely see my car in the poorly lit lot and Rosy was parked right behind in a big blacked-out Navigator like Travis's.

Just as I unlocked and opened my door, the interior lights came on, and something whizzed by my ear and shattered my Ford's windshield. Then another immediately shattered the side window near Rosy.

"Get down," Rosy heavy-whispered. "Hit the concrete like you've been shot."

I did exactly as I was told, awfully glad that Rosy was with me. He'd drawn his concealed cannon in a snap and crawled around the car and over to my side.

"Crazy bastards," Rosy heavy-whispered. "That was from a silencer. Somebody wants you dead, boy, and they almost did it. Sons-of-bitches obviously don't know you got a grade A, first-class deadeye sniper sharpshooter with you. Stay down."

I about crawled under the car and Rosy shook me.

"Be still!" he whispered as he pointed his gun toward the sound of running footsteps coming fast directly at us. "Stay down, don't move no matter what happens."

He raised up and fired three shots in the direction of the noise, and the guy coming on must've changed course on a dime because I heard like a sliding noise and shoes hitting the concrete and fading in the opposite direction.

"Dammit! Missed 'em. Should've let him get a little closer. Stay here!" Rosy ran in the direction of the fading figure and stopped abruptly when he realized a car with the lights off was speeding quickly away. "Son-of-a-bitch!"

No license plate, no nothing, but it wasn't hard to figure that Cahoone and his goons were watching my every move, and I began to wonder about Katya's safety.

I tossed the Ford's keys under the passenger seat, and made a mental note to tell the agency where it was, and that something or somebody had knocked out the windshield while I was out of town.

Grateful for my life, I let Rosy drive me to my motel. He'd called ahead and an agent was already staked out front to make sure I didn't leave earth prematurely during the night. When we arrived, he introduced me to a big guy who didn't say anything, but just grunted.

"Agent Fleming here will be parked outside your door to make sure you stay put and that nobody bothers you," Rosy explained. "He'll also drive you to the office in the morning and we'll go over the plan to put an end to the fun and games. Another agent will bring in your friend Ramon Rodriguez."

"Want to tell me about it now so I can sleep?"

"Relax, tomorrow's another day, buddy; and thank your spirit guides I met you at the 'port tonight, otherwise you'd already be genuflecting in front of Saint Peter."

I went to bed, first time in a week knowing that I was as safe as I'll ever be; but I wasn't tired because I had slept into the middle of the afternoon. I laid there and thought about whether Katya would be safe, and whether we'd ever get out of this snarled mess. If I had her here with me, I'd hold her tight and all the problems of the day would just melt away, but now they were doing everything but...

I promised myself I'd become a better man.

63 – *Got His Gun Monkeys Looking*

Right after I finally went to sleep at six a.m., somebody rapped on my door.

"Who is it?" I bellowed from bed.

"Fleming."

I leaped up and cracked the door a little, and the big guy with the shaved head said we had to leave at seven for an eight o'clock meeting. It was my turn to grunt.

I invited him in and gave him a cup of instant coffee to take back to his car while I quick-showered and shaved and tossed on yesterday's clothes. What a change, from paradise to hell in less than twenty-four hours.

On the ride in, I tried asking a few questions and all I got was grunts, so I went silent and watched the green Florida landscape rushing past my side window.

About forty minutes and forty miles from the time we left Boynton Beach, Fleming ushered me into a large sea foam green meeting room deep in DEA headquarters. Ramon was already there, the only other guy in the room.

"Why the hell didn't you tell me about this?"

"I didn't know about it myself until late last night. Sorry." I shrugged my shoulders. "I don't know any more than you do."

Right then, several guys sauntered in along with a good-looking blond wagging a pad and pencil, and right behind them Rosy Gunn and tall Travis Macintyre.

I plunked myself down next to Ramon and watched as the fed attack team scooted chairs, cleared throats, and positioned themselves ready for whatever was about to come down. Rosy and Travis took the catbird seats at each end of the long blond wood table. Ramon and I were on one side, dead center in the middle like feature attractions, or targets.

Rosy spoke first. "Word's on the street that Darragh Cahoone has put out a big contract on you, Joe; and rumor is he's got his gun monkeys looking for Ramon here. Says he wants to have a little talk."

"How do you know all this?" I held my breath, hoping there was nothing out about the cash we stashed.

"We got a low-level guy on the inside," Rosy answered. "Cahoone says he's got his reasons, but that's it."

"He's apparently hot that you screwed up his little domestic life," Travis added, "and if he stays on the loose you may actually be inside the next car that blows up, or just as bad, on the receiving end of a silent dumdum sent buzzing your way. We just don't get why he's so anxious to put you down. Can you shed a little more light on the subject?"

I shook my head slowly and fixed my mouth in the 'I have no earthly idea' pose. Crap. Darragh wants his eight million back. After taking me down he'd pump Katya just before he turned her lights off. Ramon leaned forward and raised a hand off the table like he wanted the floor.

One of the people we had not been introduced to nodded toward Ramon. "Go ahead, Mr. Rodriguez."

"The only possible reason he could want me at room temperature is because I quit pushing street drugs, unless you guys have leaked that you cut a deal with me, and with Oaks here.

"No way," Rosy said. Pushers are a dime a dozen, and we haven't leaked anything about you guys. "By the way, that was Agent Chastain who gave you the go ahead."

"Like I give a rat's ass." Ramon pulled out a cigarette.

"No smoking, Rodriguez," Chastain barked.

Ramon put his cigarette back in the package and let out a big sigh. I thought it was best to stay quiet, and not put in my dime's worth of indignation.

"Let's cut to the heart of the matter," Rosy said. "We want to use you guys to trap Cahoone and maybe some of his boys."

"Hell, yeah!" It spilled out of me. I didn't want to sound too much in favor, but I couldn't help it. Get Cahoone off the street and behind five feet of concrete, and Katya and I would be free to travel the planet and live off the eight super big with no threat of some jacko blowing us up or shooting at us. Skinny Ramon looked at me like he thought I was nuts.

"No freakin' way, José," Ramon said. "Those guys get out too quick, and they all hold grudges. Besides," he tagged, "his guys on the outside will do whatever he says. Exterminio. No way."

Ramon had a point, at least for himself. Cahoone was already trying to whack one of us. It'd only get worse for Ramon if he helped the feds.

Travis interrupted the silence. "That's official failure-to-cooperate. You signed up for this and you'll do it, or you'll be prosecuted right along with Cahoone and his thugs. Take your choice, boys."

I looked at Ramon and he looked at me for a long second. Macintyre was right, we were no longer free spirits. Either way we belonged to The Man.

"Why don't you use *your* guy?" Ramon asked.

Travis fielded that one. "We already have a role for him."

"Care to hear the plan?" Rosy gestured with an open palm to Ramon and then to me.

"Yeah, I guess," I said.

Ramon slowly shook his head from side to side. "Okay, what do we do?"

+++

The plan was simpler than I figured it would be. I was the bait, and Ramon would be the bait-seller. The feds were holding the rod and reel, and Cahoone and his guys were gonna be the bottom feeders on the hook. That is, if everything went according to the plan.

If…

64 – Bulletproof Bait

Agent Fleming drove me to the sleazy little rent-a-car store where I got the fire-balled Mustang, showed 'em his federal investigator ID, and helped me file a report. He made up a story about some vandal blowing up the gas tank and said that he'd handle the investigation with their insurance company. He told me that Rosy had already taken care of the Miami Beach police department. Anyway, they didn't want to rent me another car and I don't blame 'em. I called Avis.

Fleming dropped me off at the Lauderdale airport and I drove away in a bad ass black Lincoln with dark-tinted windows and security up the kazoo. On the way back to Boynton Beach, I stopped off at a sign-maker and a half-hour later slapped signs that said "Limousine Service" on both passenger doors. Next came a hardware store where I picked up a small can of black paint and a tiny brush. I backed up to my motel door, removed the Avis stickers, and carefully changed three digits on the plate: an S to an 8, an L to an E, and a 1 to a 4. Magic! I had a car that would be hard to track.

I committed to myself that I'd drive very carefully so as not to attract the attention of the police. I didn't want them looking too closely at the "adjustments" I'd made.

Tired, I was. Beat like a drum, so I decided to take a little siesta before the big event. The first thing I did at the motel was call Katya. There was no answer on her cell, and I tried her room. Still no answer. She was probably getting her hair done or in a noisy place where she couldn't hear her ring-tone song.

I laid down and drifted off. Yeah, I know, lay, layed, laid. Who cares?

+++

My cell phone jangled me awake. I felt my heart racing and I popped out in a cold sweat as I punched it on. It was Rosy Gunner.

"You on the move yet?"

"I just woke up."

"Listen up, Joe. Everything depends on split-second timing, so don't screw it up." Rosy sounded blunt. "Start out now, and follow the instructions exactly."

"I'll do my best," I hoped. I was beginning to feel all depressed.

We hung up and I drug myself over to the desk where I'd flopped the bulletproof vest Rosy made me put on after the meeting at DEA. I guessed it'd be the only material thing between eternity and me for the next several hours.

Travis and Rosy made us all exchange cell phone numbers, put 'em on speed-dial and test 'em before we left DEA headquarters, and we were supposed to call each other in case anything varied from the plan. My cell rang again. This time it was Ramon.

"What the hell have you gotten me into, Joe?"

"I'm the one wearing a bullet-proof vest."

"Hot news, I'm wearing one, too, only it's wired. If Cahoone suspects I'm sending sound, he'll rip the vest off me and make me eat it before he takes me out!"

"I'm sorry."

"You should be, Joe Oaks, you should be."

65 – Want to Hear My Proposal?

After I calmed things down with Ramon, I stripped the limo signs off the Lincoln and drove south to Haulover Beach just above Bal Harbour, using up the better part of an hour.

As I approached the first entrance to the park, I spotted the dark green Chevy SUV parked closest to a pier, which was part of the plan. Two men messed with rods and reels and tackle boxes.

A refreshment truck lingered in the middle of the lot with one window open. I knew that the radio guys were inside with Rosy and Travis who were armed to the teeth.

Near the edge of the water, a small fishing boat, tied to a post, was kind of bouncing in a light chop. I ignored all of 'em, as I was instructed to do. So far, everything appeared as I was told it would be.

I pulled into one of the many empty spaces at the far end of the parking lot, put on my new dark sunglasses, got out of the Lincoln, and looking all casual like a native Floridian out for a stroll, leisurely ambled toward the dock nearest the fishing boat.

So far, so good, all I had to do was mark time. So, I sat on a bench and watched, waiting for the scene to unfold.

The Miami sun was about two hours from setting, so the temperature was about perfect. I leaned back and looked up at the crystal blue sky and breathed in a deep pull of the refreshing sea air and let it out slowly. If things went haywire, it was one of the last breaths I'd ever take, but it was a delicious one.

About then, I thought of my girl Katya and wondered if she was lying outside on a Bahamian lounge chair sucking in the same great tropical air. Thinking about her hurt deeply, but I forced my mind off her and onto my job ahead. My life was now on the line.

At 4:05, after nearly thirty minutes of sitting on my duff, a black four-door with blacked out rear and side windows pulled up close to the dock. It was Cahoone's Mercedes, but he wasn't driving. I was a good fifty feet away so I squinted through my sunglasses and tried to see through the blacked-out windows and couldn't do it. The engine kept running and after less than a minute the back door opened and Ramon popped out. I tried not to notice.

He sort of casually walked up to me seated on the bench and said, "Cahoone wants to see you in the car."

That wasn't in the plan.

"No," I said. "I don't trust him. Tell him that. Tell him that he'll have to come over here to talk to me."

Ramon looked down at the asphalt and sucked his teeth. He didn't say anything, just turned and walked back to the Mercedes. The side window swooshed down about a third of the way, but I couldn't hear what Ramon said. He stood there by the driver's door like he was waiting for orders and in less than a minute the back door opened and Cahoone crawled out, but he didn't look happy. He adjusted and pulled down the tail of his rainbow-colored sport shirt, stared at me, took a breath, and walked slowly in my direction. Ramon was flanking him on the left, and Cahoone stopped and turned, and it looked like he told Ramon to go back to the car and wait, because Ramon glanced at me for a second and turned back toward the Mercedes, which rolled slowly in Ramon's direction and stopped after moving twenty or so feet.

As Cahoone closed in, the steady glare he sent my way didn't match his smile. My breathing rate stepped up and I felt a cold sweat pop out across my forehead and above my upper lip. I stood up but didn't extend my hand to shake.

"Keep your seat, Oaks."

I sat back down and he dropped and sat next to me on the bench, almost touching, which made me quite a bit nervous.

"Okay, Oaks, let's cut to it. Where's my money?"

I'd rehearsed for this and I was ready. "What money? I don't know what you're talking about."

"You know damn good and well what money; the money that walked out of my condo with your cheating little girlfriend's stuff."

"I still don't know what you're talking about. If I'd taken money from you, do you think I'd be here talkin' to you? I'm not crazy! Don't you want to hear my proposal?"

"The only proposal is, I propose you give my money back, that's the only reason I'm here, so where is it? Tell me or I'll find your little girlfriend and do what I should have done before, and if you don't tell me where the cash is, you won't live long enough to see her before I put her down."

Damn cruel ex-fake husband, and with super sensitive mics pointed right at us from the roach coach parked a few hundred feet away, I had no doubt that Rosy and Travis heard the threat and were also wondering what money Cahoone was talking about. I had to keep denying, and make the offer that the plan called for.

"Like Ramon told you, I got two million for a buy, do you want to furnish the coke, or not?"

"*Not*, asshole. You're number's up." Cahoone rose straight up, pulled down at his tropical sport shirt and walked in a rapid pace back to his car, opened the back door and slid in. I'm sure the residents could hear his door slam up in Lauderdale.

Suddenly, the car was coming toward me and gaining speed, and as the car drew even, the passenger window lowered and the barrel of a short, powerful-looking gun was pointed right at me. I didn't hear the shots, but I sure felt 'em, two or three hits in my chest knocking me backwards and knocking my breath out. I went down thinking my ribs were broken in several places, or I was dying. Last thought before I hit the ground... didn't know whether the vest saved my life or not. On the way down... got a glimpse of Rosy and another guy coming out of the refreshment truck with guns blazing at the tires and gas tank of the Mercedes. I had one last fleeting thought, wondering whether Ramon was still alive, before I went unconscious.

66 – *Where the Bullets Went In*

I came to on a bunk in the roach coach, which looked more like a combination communication center and ambulance than a refreshment truck. Two guys in white had my shirt off and were looking at where the bullets went in, or didn't *if* the so-called bulletproof vest protected me. I felt woozy, but after a half-minute or so, got up the strength to ask questions.

"Was I hit?" I was trying to gulp in enough air, but couldn't seem to do it.

"Were you hit? Oh, man, were you ever hit. You got grazed on the head by one slug, and you took at least three in the chest. You got some badly bruised ribs," said the blond-haired, youngest of the two guys. He took my left hand and guided it up to my head. I felt the bandage.

He went on, "That's where you got grazed. Lucky for you, you had on the Kevlar. Two of the slugs almost penetrated the entire twenty-eight layers."

"My friend Ramon–"

"The DEA guys have him.

"Did they catch–"

"Yeah, the cops laid out spike strips at all the exits and our men had already knocked out the gas tank and one tire, so the guys who shot at you only got about three blocks. That's all I know."

"--Am I okay to leave, I mean drive?"

"Sure, no permanent damage, and if you comb your hair just right you can even cover up the place where you got grazed. You are one lucky bass."

+++

As I exited Haulover on the way back to Boynton Beach, I dialed Katya. She answered on the first ring. After making sure she was okay, I unloaded my off-the-cuff scheme for our next few moves.

"I can't tell you anything now, but you're not safe. Are you dressed?"

"Yes, I was going to dinner." Her voice sounded strained. "What's happening wi–"

I interrupted. "Grab what you can't leave behind, stuff it in a small bag and head for the airport. Take the next available flight to Miami and call me with your arrival time."

"What about all my clothes and new things I got with my winnings?"

"I'll make sure they get packed and put on a flight tonight, and I'll settle the bill by phone, so don't stop at the front desk. I'll meet you at the arrival entrance, not at luggage. Look for a black Lincoln sedan with blacked-out windows. Got it?"

"Joe, are you okay? Are you–"

I cut her off. "I'll be okay when I see you in Miami."

67 – This Sumbitch Is Still Alive?

Next on my hot list, find out if the Cahoone threat was still looming large. I called Rosy on his cell, and he told me about the take down.

"Didn't go exactly according to plan though," Rosy explained. "We nailed him for first degree attempted homicide instead of dealing snow.

"Yeah, I've got bruised ribs and a new part in my hair to prove it."

"Sorry 'bout that. Goes with the territory. But the medic said it was minor." Rosy changed subjects. "Uh, what money was Cahoone talking about?"

"I have no idea. He's got a lot of traffic through his condo." I acted cool and unconcerned. "I guess somebody helped themselves. Where's Cahoone *now*?"

"You're gonna be a lot safer, pal." Rosy sounded proud of himself when he told me. "He's being held with no bail along with his two thugs who used you for target practice. Didn't get his second-in-command though, Louie Ladue is still out there, so be careful."

"How about Ramon Rodriguez, is he–?"

"Probably on his way home."

"What's next for me?"

"Can't say for sure, except sit tight, you may have to testify. Stay where we can reach you."

"In Florida?"

"You got it."

+++

When Rosy told me Darragh Cahoone was in the slammer, a ton of poundage lifted off my shoulders, and the stuff rushing through my brain slowed down. I took a deep, healing breath of salt air and called Ramon's cell.

"Yo, Joe, you still alive, you sumbitch?" Ramon actually sounded like his old self.

"Yeah, unfortunately for you, you drugged up pothead." I couldn't help dropping back into my own old ways, considering the release from what I'd just been through. "What the hell went wrong anyway?" I asked.

"I played it like I was supposed to. Cahoone said he was interested in doing the big deal with you and I was supposed to be part of the meeting since I was wired, but I guess he planned to knock you off instead. He probably would have taken me out, too, *if* you hadn't refused to meet in his car. Lucky stroke for you, *and* me."

"That's the second time I've heard that today."

"Lucky for you, make it the third. Glad to know you're okay, Joe-balls."

"Hold on a second." A text came in from Katya giving her flight number and arrival time.

"I need to celebrate. You dating anyone?" I asked.

"Oh, yeah, a cute little waitress who loves my boys."

"Well, keep you pants on, Ramon, and let's celebrate our butts off tonight."

"We gotta stay outta sight. Cahoone's got gun monkeys running all over the place."

"How about a hotel suite?"

"Yeah, South Beach, about nine o'clock."

"Text me the address. I'm picking up Katya, so bring your girlfriend and some good stuff."

+++

Katya exited the terminal looking perfect as usual, and carrying nothing but her makeup bag and purse; so I relaxed a little, knowing that a tail, if there were one, wouldn't suspect she'd bolt for the airport leaving all her stuff behind. She seemed down, almost irritable. I guess rushing to catch a plane and hiking through long buildings numbed her for my little welcome kiss and hug.

On the way into South Beach, I called the Atlantis and told the front desk to pack up all Katya's stuff and send it by overnight air, and to add a hundred dollar tip to the tab. Then I updated her on everything that had happened. She listened intently, but made no comment. I guess she was trying to shake off the hurried flight.

Anyway, I said it was time to chill out and hang loose, if only for one night.

68 – Rowdy Came In and Said Howdy

Ramon picked a snazzy art deco hotel with a four star French restaurant on the low end of Ocean Drive, and reserved a suite on the top floor. It was not cheap, but it had twenty-four hour room service.

None of us except Ramon's girlfriend, Neela, had eaten since breakfast, so we ordered from the downstairs oo-la-la French bistro. While we waited, everybody did a couple of lines to set the mood, and Katya acted like she didn't want to, but did anyway.

A half-hour of increasingly fast small talk later, room service rolled in two carts containing horses' doovers, appetizers and soups, and said they'd be back in twenty minutes with the main courses.

Neela tugged at Ramon's blue suede jacket sleeve.

"I need some more candy," she said. "I want some more candeeee!"

Ramon pulled her fingers off his jacket and brushed up the suede with his other hand. "Wait 'til after we get our steaks and stuff, Neela."

"Oh kaaay."

Katya looked at Neela and scrunched up her already pouty lips, Katya's way of showing disapproval. Neela ignored her, if she was even aware that Katya was giving her the once-over.

Young Neela was no wallflower, so Polish supermodel Katya, which is the way Katya insisted I introduce her, obviously considered Neela inferior.

Maybe if we got hopped up enough, good ol' Catherine Lucille Bobo would come out and play. I tested. "Catherine Lucille?" I said to my soup.

"Who?" Katya replied in her annoyed tone.

I slurped another spoonful. "Oh, somebody I used to know made a soup that tasted like this."

"Well, it's kinda strange saying her name out of the blue."

"Just somebody I used to know. No big deal." That was sort of a challenge, and I shouldn't have said it, because from that point on, Katya was cool as a cucumber toward me.

I thought, 'what the hell', and I joined in with Neela and pushed Ramon for a couple more hits, to which he obliged being outnumbered two to one, and he himself caved and took a pop.

Well, rowdy came in and said 'howdy'. We were off and running like three racehorses on speed. If Katya wanted to be a spectator, she was allowed.

Ramon started to light up a joint.

"Hey, don't. Let's not stink up the place until after we get our main courses." I said.

"I agree." Ramon put the weed away and snorted another line. Neela followed, and so did I.

We three proceeded to solve the problems of the world in a constant stream of chatter with Katya looking on, until the knock at the door and the arrival of the two tuxedo clad waiters with the balance of our dinners. Ramon signed the tab and the two waiters, one old hand and one apprentice type, left the suite.

"I don't know whether you noticed, but the young guy took a long look at the stuff you left out," Katya said.

I jerked my head around, and sure enough, coke was laid out in three perfect lines on the coffee table.

"Don't worry about it," Ramon said, again pulling the packet from his jacket and extracting a true fatty. "Those guys see it every day. This is South Beach, man!" He lit the cigar size doobie and handed it to Neela, who took a deep hit and passed it to me.

"Excuse me, please." Katya got up from the table and looked like she might be headed toward the Little Girl's Room. I guessed it was time to freshen her makeup.

"You're excused," we all said in near unison. She stopped behind my chair.

"Where you goin', hon?" I asked.

"Down to the bar and some fresh air. I don't want to get high tonight."

"There's a mini-bar in the other room," Ramon pointed over his shoulder.

"I really want a chocolate martini."

"No can do," I turned and shrugged. "Don't got the fixin's."

She leaned over and gave me a hug from the back. "I'll just be a half-hour or less."

"I'm too wasted to go down with you."

"I know, Joe-baby. Have a good time. I'll be back before you know it." She turned and left.

The party was gettin' good, and it had been weeks since I'd tied one on.

69 – *Just My Usual Brick*

It was a good thing Katya left when she did, because not more than ten minutes later, the Miami Beach police busted into the room with the night manager right behind 'em objecting and yelling.

"You don't have the right to disturb our guests. I'm going straight to the mayor in the morning!" he yowled.

Ramon, Neela, and I were now standing bolt upright with our mouths open

"Go ahead and report us," the burley police sergeant answered. "Your guests are the ones making the complaint."

A new arrival, a short guy in a dark suit, rushed in like he was late for a plane. His ID badge read *Security*. The hotel manager whipped around to face him.

"Where've you been? Did you get a call about this?" he asked.

"I did, I couldn't find you. Somebody complained about noise and the smell."

One of the officers, not part of the discussion, and wearing blue rubber gloves, strolled around the suite picking up Ramon's bag of goodies, assorted roaches, and the other paraphernalia that we'd been snorting, toking and choking on. Shithouse mouse.

I observed my life crumbling in front my eyes. The lead cop told Ramon and Neela to sit down, and he looked over his shoulder at me and barked, "You, too!"

"Yes, sir," I said as my cell vibrated in my pocket. It was Katya. I answered, trying to think of something to say that wouldn't attract attention to the conversation. I went lame for a moment.

"Hi," I whispered.

"Joe, baby, do you want me to bring you a few shots of your favorite bourbon?"

"Listen," I cupped the phone to keep my side of the conversation confidential. "The police are here. You stay downstairs until we know what's happening. Keep your phone on and I'll call you back." I hung up and toddled over to the sofa and sat down with Ramon and Neela.

Ramon was already cuffed with plastic ties, and I think I know why. While I was on the phone with Katya, I watched a stout Hispanic cop spot Ramon in the bedroom trying to shove his coat of many pockets under the mattress. Too bad for Ramon, because not only did it conceal copious amounts of Maui wowee and birdie powder, it also contained his wallet and identification. I was clean, not carrying any dope; so I kept my mouth shut and played the part of *just a user.*

"You people," the top cop said, "have an abnormal amount of illegal drugs, and we're taking you in for questioning.

"Does that mean we're un..." I started to ask.

"Yes sir, you three are officially under arrest." He read our Miranda rights that I had damn near memorized from hearing on television so many times.

"And today started out being such a great day," Ramon said as he shook his head and fixed his eyes on the art deco carpet. Neela meanwhile was whimpering into her dinner napkin.

Me? I was just normally shitting my usual brick.

Katya had money left, I was sure, from her casino winnings, but I had to get the motel and car keys to her without her being implicated in the mess. I turned to the cop giving the orders.

"I have to settle up with the manager before you take us in. Will that be okay?"

"Sure, go ahead." What else could he say? 'No' I suppose, but he was a nice cop.

I motioned the hotel night manager to the corner of the room and I took out my wallet and keys. I counted out ten crispies and handed him the thousand, along with the keys to the Lincoln and the Boynton Beach motel.

"Please give these keys to Katya Cahoone. She's downstairs in the bar. Short blond hair, beautiful, and wearing a tan dress. Let me know if you can't find her." I scribbled my cell phone number on a scrap of paper from my pocket and handed it to him with the ten one-hundred-dollar bills. "Will this cover the suite and dinner?"

"I'm sure it will, Mr. uh–"

"Oaks, Joe Oaks. What's your name?"

"Benson. Herbert Benson." I made a mental note.

I called Katya, gave her the night manager's name and filled her in before the cops made me empty my pockets, cuff me behind my back, and cram all three of us into the backseat of the squad car.

The six-block trip to the Miami Beach police station took less than five minutes, but time enough for me to figure out what to do next, if and when I could use a phone. I had to call Rosy and tell him the truth.

70 – Waiting for the Next Disaster

Inside the swanky police headquarters, the arresting officer snipped off our plasticuffs and told us to sit down and be patient, and that processing would only take a few minutes.

After a half-hour that seemed much longer, Ramon was booked for felony possession of illegal drugs, described as approximately an eight-ounce glass of marijuana and approximately four tablespoons of cocaine. He was also booked for contributing to the delinquency of a minor, Neela being only eighteen.

"I didn't know!" Ramon yelped.

"Well, you shoulda," the desk sergeant calmly said. "Just because somebody looks nineteen or older doesn't mean she is."

Ramon got his one telephone call to his plainclothes contact and asked for help; but, according to Ramon, he said "no deal, too much evidence."

"This is all your fault, Joe Oaks," Ramon whispered loud enough for everyone in the room to hear. "You're the one who wanted a stupid celebration."

"Quiet over there!" the desk sergeant yelled, interrupting his phone call with Neela's daddy. I overheard him say she was being sent over to the Juvenile Detention Center in Miami.

A few moments later, a muscular female cop with a butch haircut stopped in front of Neela and rattled her squad car keys.

"Come on, young lady." She bent down and grasped Neela's elbow, pulling her up from the bench. "I'm your taxi to detention. Yo' papa is on his way and we don't want to keep yo' papa waitin'."

Neela let out a long pained wail that sounded more teenage than woman, and a couple of moments later she was gone, leaving Ramon and me sitting and staring, and waiting for the next disaster to strike.

I got my one dinky telephone call and Rosy grumbled that I interrupted his beauty sleep, but I could tell from his voice that he must've sat straight up when I told him where Ramon and I were.

While I was giving him the rundown, he kept saying, "Oh, dammit, what's next?" He showed up forty minutes later, and he did not look happy. His one glance at us confirmed that unsavory visual tidbit.

He went straight to the cop who'd been barking orders, showed his high mucky-muck ID, and the cop handed him the papers he'd been working on. Rosy perused them, one swift page at a time, glancing disgustedly in our direction between pages. After a minute or so, he passed the report back to the cop and tromped over to our bench and sat down in a chair opposite us.

A younger cop, guarding us from a few feet away, cast a wary eye and Rosy sighed, reached in his pocket, yanked out his wallet and flashed his badge. The young cop glimpsed it, nodded at Rosy and looked away.

Rosy didn't talk right away, maybe trying to decide how hard to smack us with the facts. Then he looked directly at me and drilled right in with those black eyes.

"Mr. Oaks, you've got a problem." He switched his stare to Ramon. "Mr. Rodriguez, you've got a much bigger problem." Neither of us said anything, so Rosy continued. "Your 'no prosecution' agreements stated if you participated in the sale, acquisition, *or use of* illegal drugs or controlled substances, that your agreements would be null and void. Didn't you read the fine print?"

I answered, "Yeah, I read it. I just didn't think we'd be caught."

Ramon looked down and nodded.

"Both you guys are facing heavy charges."

Ramon was first to react. "What if I still testify on Cahoone?"

"You, reduced a little, maybe… slim chance," he said to Ramon.

"What about me?" I was practically holding my breath.

Rosy thought a moment. "Reduced, maybe. In the meantime, we're gonna let the State of Florida make sure that you two stay out of trouble. They'll be moving you to County in an hour or so. You'll find out about bail possibilities over there."

"Isn't there any way," I pleaded, "that you can–"
Rosy interrupted, "I'll think about it, Oaks."

I held my breath again while Rosy appeared to be pondering. Not more than one second later he looked up and nodded.

"I thought about it long and hard, and… no."

+++

Ramon and I were shuffled into the back of a piss-fragrant wagon and sent over to Miami-Dade County Jail. Just before we were transported, Rosy left after speaking with some guys in the back that I hadn't seen before, and one of them came forward and told us we'd learn about the full charges against us at our court appearance and arraignment in the morning. Crap in a basket.

Nothing made sense anymore.

71 – *Some Kind of Glop*

I vegetated; awake for the balance of the night, all three hours of it, propped up on a hard slab of a bed with my back against a concrete block wall. Everything in my cell was gray with a little stainless steel here and there.

At 6:00 a.m., a guy with a badge shoved a breakfast tray through a slot, designed I guess, for giving meals to the jailbirds. The tray sported some kind of glop in the center, an orange, and coffee. The badge also shoved a matching orange jumpsuit through the bars and told me to put it on and to hand him my own clothes, which he'd put with my cell phone and other stuff. He also gave me a verbal schedule.

My appearance and arraignment were set for eight-thirty and I was told we'd be leaving for court promptly at seven. I assumed Ramon would be in the same group.

Sure enough, at 6:55 a deputy opened my cell and escorted me to the van, and waiting inside was a load of orange suits--Ramon, with a couple of scraggly-looking guys from gutter city, and a row of assorted black dudes lining the bench on the other side. The black guys were all shackled, hand and foot, to one another--one long row--and the deputy chained me to Ramon, who was already attached to the scraggs.

Ramon didn't say a word during the trip, and the couple of times I commented he completely ignored me. I guess I had it coming.

+++

We were guided out of the van, into the courthouse, and down the hall into a holding cell where we waited not more than five minutes.

Two armed deputies, both big hulks, unlocked Ramon and me, and escorted us up an elevator, down a hall, and into the courtroom, where we were shown the way to our seats.

They called Ramon's case first, and he got on his feet and walked forward to where the deputy directed him to stand before the judge. I had to strain to hear what the judge was saying, and the list was long and included felony first-degree drug charges, but the two biggies were drug trafficking and contributing to the delinquency of a minor. He reminded Ramon that he had faced similar charges twice before.

Next, he read Ramon his rights: *'You have the right to an attorney. If you cannot afford one, one will be appointed. You have the right to confront and cross-examine witnesses against you. You have the right to a jury trial. You have the right to not incriminate yourself. You have the right to a speedy trial. If you plead guilty, you could be sentenced up to thirty years in prison. Do you understand these rights?'*

The judge asked Ramon if he had an attorney and he said yes and that he had not called him, but would do so as soon as he was allowed. The judge affirmed that Ramon would be held in jail without bail until his trial. I heard Ramon expel air like somebody had knocked the breath out of him.

Hulk number one escorted Ramon out of the courtroom and presumably back to his cell. Next, the female bailiff called my name and hulk number two ushered me up front to face the judge. I felt myself go weak when he read exactly the same charges for me, minus delinquency of a minor. The Miami Beach police probably established that Neela was Ramon's girlfriend. I remember her telling a cop that she never saw me until the party, and that she was dating Ramon.

Anyway when the judge got to the part about up to thirty years in prison and setting my bail at fifty thousand dollars, I got dizzy. I remember saying "yes" to the judge's question about understanding my rights, and that I didn't have an attorney, but would get one if I could have my cell phone for a few minutes. Then I hit my head on the stone floor, out cold, or so the bailiff said.

72 – It's Just a Piece of Paper

I woke up in a dark windowless space, a cross between a cell and a tiny hospital room, and I had a headache the size of a watermelon.

The sound of keys rattling and of a lock turning drew my sight to the heavy door into my room swinging open and hissing shut behind the intruder.

The guy in white brought my phone to me and laid it on the nightstand. "The judge said to give this to you so you can call an attorney."

"Where am I?"

"County Jail infirmary. You got a bad concussion. Bailiff said you passed out and hit your head on the stone floor."

"Can anybody visit me in here?"

"Naw, but when you get back to your cell you can have visitors. No many though. Wife, girlfriend, child, lawyer, like that."

I reached for my phone. "Would you mind? I need to make a call."

"No problem." The deputy or orderly, or whatever he was, turned around on his way out. "Remember, if you need anything, all you got to do is yell out. We can hear everything that's going on in the room at all times." He winked and exited, and I heard the click of the lock after the automatic door shut behind him.

I hit the speed dial for Katya. God, how I love that woman, but all I got was her dial tone song, and at the moment I didn't feel like dancing all night.

"Katya, call me as soon as you pick up this message." I didn't want to give any extra info to whoever might be tuned in.

Next, I searched the phone's memory and punched redial for Rosy Gunn. He answered right away.

"Well, Joe Oaks, I thought that I might be hearing from you again."

"Help me get out of here."

"No can do, my friend."

"Why?" I felt a quick swirl of bitter acid fill my stomach and rush up my throat.

"Your immunity agreement, no coverage for new felonies; but worse, since you and your pal violated the terms, we're also obligated to file against both of you."

"–For?" I already knew.

"For trafficking and distributing illegal drugs to personnel of federally licensed radio stations, and for selling phony prescription drugs. However, if you're still willing to help us put Cahoone away for a few decades, we'll swing."

"What about Ramon?"

"Your friend Ramon is in deeper trouble. He's in for a long, long time--a lot longer than you. When he realizes how long, he ain't gonna be cooperating with the friends of the guys that are pushing for thirty years."

"You gave me your word. It's on paper, signed; no prosecution." My life was fizzling, evaporating.

"If you stayed out of trouble. Besides, in Florida, there a little thing called Rachel's Law. It says we're not obligated to give an informant a reduced sentence. It was on the news. Have your lawyer check it out."

"I don't have a lawyer."

Rosy didn't say anything for a few seconds. Then he cleared his throat and told me something else that I already knew.

"Well, you better get one."

73 – *She Just Hung Up*

I'd been lying in the dark with my cracked head throbbing for the better part of three hours when my cell phone gave off that special tone that I'd set up for Katya's incoming calls. What a relief. A few hours ago, I was dying or dead as far as the world was concerned; hell, as far as I was concerned–and now my doll Katya would be coming to my rescue. I snatched the phone off the nightstand and answered.

"Hi, doll baby."

"Joe, where are you? Where have you been?"

"Listen carefully. I'm in County Jail Infirmary, and I'm okay. I'm not sure, but I think I remember they set my bail at $50,000. You got to bail me out. There's more, there's lots more, but I've got to get out first."

She didn't say anything for a long time.

"Katya?"

"Yeah, I'm here. I'm thinking."

"Can you do it? Or should I get a lawyer?"

"--I'll handle it, Joe. Don't worry. I'll get you out." She hung up.

I wanted to say more, but she just hung up. Anyway, the eavesdroppers were listening in and probably recorded everything. Screw 'em.

+++

A few hours later, the pain in my head eased up, and I actually felt like moving around, as much as anyone can move around in a eight-by-ten space. While I was stretching and trying to get my blood flowing, a guard slipped a food tray in the slot by the door and hit what sounded like a desk bell a couple of times. I guess that was to let me know dinner had arrived, either that or train me to salivate like Pavlov's dog. Arf, arf.

Anyway, while I was supping on the County's rich vittles, a glop of hash and a hunk of bread, a burly Hispanic guard I'd never seen unlocked my door and propped it open.

"You're free to leave, señor, you've been bailed out. Your ride is waiting for you at the front entrance. Here are your clothes; sign right here."

So, just like that, I'm out.

I looked at the guard a moment, and took the clipboard he was holding out and the bag containing some of my personal stuff. I found the line on the form and scribbled my name.

"Is the person waiting for me a pretty blond lady?"

"I dunno, I didn't see. I was just told to let you out and walk you to the front. I'll wait outside while you get dressed."

I couldn't wait to strip off the jailbird clothes … never looked good in orange. I dressed as fast as I could, grabbed my phone and stuffed my pockets with my other crap and pushed open the unlocked door of my mini-cell. Somebody still had my wallet and keys.

The big guard nodded his massive head and his mop of black greasy hair flopped forward. "Follow me, señor."

I had made up my mind what I was gonna do, and Katya had better be ready.

+++

"She put up the bail in your name." The releasing deputy, a two hundred pound, muscled female, complete with muscles in her fingers, pushed the paper at me for my signature. "That means if you don't skip you'll get most of your money back after the trial, or if charges are dropped."

"I hope--" I left my wishful thought hanging as I signed and pushed the paper back at the woman who could pick me up and throw me across the room at about thirty miles an hour if she wanted to.

She reached under the counter and produced the remains of my captive life, an envelope containing my ID and wallet, and handed them to me with a smile.

"You're free to go, Mr. Oaks."

I nodded and walked toward the front door while extracting stuff from the envelope and reorganizing my life, cramming the evidence of it back into my coat pockets.

I began to think how amazing freedom is, and how easy it is to lose it.

74 – *If I Had a Life Left*

The black Lincoln with the dark windows sat in the Passenger Loading Zone, but I couldn't see inside. My heart beat faster with every step, and I couldn't wait to touch Katya, to kiss her, to hold her tight and not let go, and to pop the question for the umpteenth and last time. Last, because if she didn't say 'yes' today, I'd have to get over it and get on with my life, if I had one left after the upcoming trial.

I grabbed the passenger door handle and pulled the door open, and there she sat, in the driver's seat all smiling and dimples. My heart leaped nearly out of my chest to see her in an almost skin tight tropical print with greens and reds and lavender flowers, and birds of every color. Her lipstick matched her shoes and the red in her dress, and her perfect hair framed the most beautiful, most precious face I'd ever seen. This woman was everything I hoped for; and here she was, about to be mine if she accepted my proposal.

I tossed the empty envelope over the headrest into the back seat.

"Geeze, I missed you, baby doll." I slid in. "You driving, or you want me to take over?"

"You've been through enough, Joe. Relax and I'll keep the wheel."

I leaned over the center console and kissed Katya's cheek. She showed dimples and let out a little soft laugh, but kept her eyes on the street.

"Where're we headed? You hungry?" I asked.

"No. You?"

"I had a tray a few minutes ago."

"A tray?"

"In jail. They dump everything on a metal tray and shove it at you."

"I didn't know and I don't ever intend to see it."

Katya's priorities were straight.

"They're probably watching my every move, doll baby, so we still can't go near the banks. How much do we have left?"

"There's thirty-three thousand in your suitcase. I spread it out so there are no bulges in the lining." Dear Katya, thinking ahead, another reason why I love her so.

"That should be enough for an attorney."

"They've got to put Darragh away, put him away for the rest of his life," she said. "He tried to kill you! I'll go state's evidence with you. I'll tell them everything I know."

The unselfish willingness from my precious doll made my heart seize up and squeeze. I believed with every fiber of my being that Katya's testimony would earn me a ticket to freedom and salt ol' Darragh Cahoone away where he could never hurt us.

If this is what love is, I am sick in love from the ground to the top of my head and everything in between.

"Okay. Here's my titanic moment," I announced with a flourish befitting only an actor about to play the biggest, most important part of his life. "Here it comes…"

"Go ahead and ask me, Joe, so I can say 'yes'!"

Well, that took me quite a bit by surprise. I'm sure my jaw hit the floorboard of the Lincoln. Here's this luscious, blond doll-baby of a woman leading me into saying what I want to say, and giving me her answer in advance.

"Will you... will you marry me, Katya, Catherine Lucille?"

"Joe?"

Uh, oh. Surprise time. Probably 'no for now', or 'I will after you get out of prison' or...

Thank heaven, there was nobody behind us because Katya slammed on the brakes and looked at me square on. She smiled and said, "Yes, yes, Joe. I will."

I leaned over the console and pulled her into me and we kissed for what seemed an eternity and I drew into me her fragrance of flowers and candy-and love.

After the kiss to last a lifetime, I leaned back and just looked at my doll. She was so beautiful and I was so drained. After the buildup in my mind, after worrying out all the possible outcomes, my dream proposal came out perfectly, just the way I wanted it to be.

"If you didn't ask me, I was gonna ask you," my doll said. "And I knew *you'd* say 'yes', so I've already planned where I want our honeymoon, but I'm going to save it as a surprise until I get back."

"Until... what?"

"Until I get back from Detroit. I've got to tell my folks, and I want to do it in person; not on some old cold telephone call."

Well, sure. A woman has got to do woman things, or girl-girl things, I reasoned. I'd miss her like hell, but a marriage is about compromise.

"How long will–"

"Just a couple of days, Joe-baby. Just a couple of days."

+++

We got a sack of assorted Taco Bell delicacies in Boynton Beach and stowed away in our motel room for the night, and what a night; the very best night of my life. She loved me in ways I'd never been loved before. An off-the-charts consummation of marriage before the marriage! We did things with the human body that I didn't know were possible.

At two o'clock in the morning, we finally fell asleep in each other's arms, and it was the best sleep I'd ever had in my entire life.

75 - *Right Over My Heart*

I shook off sleep three hours before Katya's flight, and shaved and dressed and watched my gorgeous doll get ready, so I'd have a fresh memory of her doing all her feminine things, dressing and stuff, to last me until she returned from Detroit. I honestly didn't think I could make it without her for two whole days.

We left in plenty of time and I drove slowly on the way to the airport stealing glances at the beautiful woman in the passenger seat who would soon be my wife.

"What time's your return flight?" She'd already booked everything and picked up her itinerary from a kiosk at the motel while I picked up breakfast.

"Oh, Joe, I've told you three times, meet me about ten minutes after noon at US Air baggage claim. If there's any change, I'll call you on your cell. Okay, sweetheart?"

"Day after tomorrow, ten after noon. I just wanted to make sure I got it right. It's gonna be pretty lonely." I was already feeling empty, like a big hollow space was somehow appearing and enlarging just below my heart and reaching down into my whole lower body. I must've shown it, because Katya kept her eyes on my drooping face and she read me just right.

"I'll be at my mother's or my sister's," she said. "And you're gonna be just fine. It's only two days."

"Give me their numbers so I can call you."

Katya gave me kind of a sweet smile, and took a beat before rummaging through her purse for a pen and something to write on.

"Here," she said, handing me their numbers.

I stuffed the folded scrap of paper deep in my shirt pocket right over my heart and patted it secure.

She went quiet for a while and seemed to drop into deep thought. I let her have her space.

This morning, I'd also decided to spend the next forty-eight hours on my immediate future doing whatever possible to help me be free for Katya and our life together.

She broke her silence. "You're a decent guy, Joe. You don't belong around certain people."

I let a few seconds pass. "Ramon?"

She didn't reply, but she knew I felt guilty about his *for-all-practical-purposes* forthcoming lifetime sentence, and that there was little I could do. So I made up my mind right then and there not to stress about Ramon, or to try to contact him. What was happening to him was the result of his entire past, not just my little window of time with him. He'd been dealing drugs most of his life, and I guess he'd be paying for it with the rest of it.

Shithouse mouse, I was lucky to get out of the business before it ate me alive.

We drove into the departing passengers area, and I got out and opened the car door for Katya and unloaded the luggage for the skycap. She handed him her ticket and pulled me back toward the car for a long lingering kiss, into which I melted.

She pushed me away. "Now, just go, and don't make me look back or I'll cry," she said.

I honored her wishes, watched her prance her way back to the skycap that was holding her ticket out in her direction. She snatched it out of his hand and pranced into the terminal. She never turned back in my direction, and that was okay with me–or *I* would have cried.

76 - Into Places I'd Never Been

The trip from Miami International to Boynton Beach took a lifetime, or seemed like it. Without Katya I felt empty, drifting, kind of weird in the stomach in a lonely sort of way, until my cell phone vibrated. I fumbled it and answered the incoming call from Travis Macintyre.

"Joe, a question's come up. I want to caution you that whatever you say can be used against you. Understand?"

"Yeah."

"The issue is your bail money. Where'd you get it? Where'd it come from?"

I hadn't fully thought that out in advance, and the long pause after Travis asked the question probably was making me look pretty suspicious. Then I said something dumb.

"I don't know. Savings, I guess."

"Savings? You guess?"

"–My girlfriend, her savings. I owe her plenty."

"The Cahoone girl?"

"Yeah."

He took a short pause. "Okay, it was just a question." Then a longer pause. "Good enough. Stick around close so we can reach you."

"Wait. I got a question myself."

"Go ahead."

The most important few words of my life were about to be presented to one Agent Macintyre, and I had to get 'em just right.

"Travis, I want to help put Cahoone away for the rest of his life, and the same for his friends. If I do my part, will you help me get off? Really get off? I want to be a good citizen, raise a family, be a normal guy."

I held my breath waiting for a response, and finally Travis made a grunting noise before coming back.

"I'll talk to Rosy. No promises though."

"Thanks, I appreciate it." I didn't beg. I presented my plea. That was all I could do.

+++

I completed the drive to Boynton, parked the car, let myself in the room, and flopped down on the bed. About now, Katya would be arriving in Detroit. I never had somebody I loved flying around without me, so I had to know if her flight arrived safely. I called information for US Air's number and dialed it, and punched Operator until I got a live one.

"Did the flight from Miami to Detroit arrive on time?" A few seconds later I got my relief; the agent said it arrived ten minutes early. I decided to give Katya time for greetings and hugs, and to get to her mother's place before I called. My heart was actually hurting. My first time to be this deeply in love had legs of its own, and they were leading me into places I'd never been.

While lying on the bed where we made love for most of last night, I recreated the peak moments until I relaxed and smiled at the feelings and images, moving, gyrating, pulsing in my mind. I fell asleep.

77 - I Just Couldn't Help It

When I awoke, the sun was lower in the sky, sending a shaft of luminous yellow through the window's sheer drape. Glittering dust particles moved slowly in the brilliant light as my awareness came on line. I looked at my watch. I'd been asleep almost two hours. Way longer than I intended.

I sat up quickly in bed, dug into my pants pocket for my cell phone, and hit Katya's speed dial number.

There was a long pause, and then I got a recorded operator that said something about it not being a working number. So I dialed it again, and after a little pause, got the same thing. She probably forgot to pay the bill since the phone was working yesterday.

I felt in my shirt pocked for the paper with Katya's family phone numbers, pulled it out, unfolded it and smoothed it out on the bed. I carefully punched in her mother's telephone number, checking each digit as I input it on the phone's tiny screen against Katya's handwriting.

A gruff sounding guy answered, and I asked for Catherine Lucille.

"There's no one here by that name."

"Is this the Bobo residence?" I began to breathe shallow and a little rapid.

"Who? Naw. Wrong number!" He hung up.

I sat on the edge of the bed with the phone to my ear, not believing what I just heard. No, something is wrong with my dialing or–

I tried the alternate number, Katya's sister. There it was on the paper in Katya's own handwriting. It rang four times and an answering device picked up and a male voice made an announcement.

"You've reached Tony's Plumbing. If you have an emergency or you'd like to schedule a maintenance appointment, leave your name and number and we'll return your call within an hour." Katya's sister was supposed to be a single girl who lived alone.

By then I was sick, really sick, feeling like I was about to throw up; but I forced the urge down and took a deep breath. There were two other things I had to do, had to do right now.

I searched through the notes in my coat pockets and found Herbert Benson's telephone number; Benson, the South Beach hotel manager I talked to before I was arrested. He answered right away and I asked him who made the complaint about the noise and the smell coming from our suite the night we were arrested. He said it was not from a hotel line, and that the call was made directly to 911. He further said the police told him that the trouble call came from a cell phone inside the hotel.

I hesitated before I asked. "Did the police identify the number?"

"If they did, they didn't tell me; but the captain did say that when they called back to verify location, all they got was a weird karaoke version of 'I Could Have Danced All Night'.

I couldn't speak because of the fist-size lump in my throat, so I hung up and sat in the spot of sun on the edge of the bed for I don't know how long.

I tried to be a man about things, but no matter how hard I tried on this one, tears still leaked out and flowed down my face. I just couldn't help it.

I dragged myself to the bathroom, splashed a little cold water around my eyes and cheeks and toweled off. One last question burned in my mind, but I already knew the answer.

I had four banks to hit between Delray Beach and West Palm, and I had an hour-and-a-half before closing.

+++

I felt like an empty shell, no, like a dead husk, during my mindless drive between banks.

My worst fears were true. All four safety-deposit boxes were empty. A note in Katya's handwriting was in the bottom of the box in West Palm Beach.

"Sorry, Joe. --Kat"

+++

Thursday morning, I drove slowly to Miami International and by noon I was standing in front of US Airways baggage.

I waited an hour-and-a-half after every last female passenger picked up her luggage from the arriving Detroit flight.

I had to give her, and myself, that one last chance.

78 - *In Several Hundred Years*

The next several months passed, and with each day I recovered a smidgen more of my self-respect, but at that rate it would take several hundred years to put ol' Joe back together. Resigned to my fate, I ate and slept, and stayed scarce to everyone except the DEA guys. Whenever they called, I delivered whatever they wanted; and by mid-fall, my testimony, along with that which was coerced out of Ramon Rodriguez, had put Darragh Cahoone so deep into a Federal penitentiary that he probably wished he'd gotten the death penalty. The feds gave Ramon a reduced sentence; fifteen years, shaving a full decade-and-a-half off his scorecard. That meant he'd be eligible for parole in twelve years and three months, which included the time he'd already been in the clink.

I fared much better. I got off as a first time offender with time served, two years parole, and a five thousand dollar fine. My Miami lawyer with the funny name, Justin Kase, said he was a bargain for a fee of only twenty thousand simoleons, which took all my available cash except for enough to scrape by on until the court returned forty-two thousand five-hundred of the fifty grand bail.

Also, I finally got around to closing out my California apartment; and with my reputation shot to hell for promoting pop music, I looked around for another way to make a living, but found the job market in sad shape, matching me perfectly.

79 - *Share My Story?*

Saturday afternoon in mid-October on one of those perfect South Florida days, I drove around with the top down on my new, actually old, Mustang that I bought outright for a few grand off a used car lot. I almost bought a Toyota, but I realized that every time I got into it I'd think of Katya, not something I wanted to do, especially since figuring out that she, and perhaps a former Cahoone lieutenant she was conning, maybe Louie himself, were somehow behind the shootout at the airport and my first little black Mustang turning into a fireball a few weeks ago.

Anyway, I was enjoying the perfect Florida sunshine when I passed a mega-church on Biscayne Boulevard with one of those big reader board signs stuck out near the street. I read the message twice before it sunk in.

"Share Your Story, Validate Yourself, Meet New Friends. 11 AM Sunday"

Well, God knows I got a story to share, and sure as hell needed a new set of friends. I decided to show up Sunday morning and start a new life.

At least I'd investigate the possibility.

80 - Heavenly Chops

Sunday morning at ten-thirty I parked my new-old Mustang in the church parking lot and trudged up the steps with a bit of dread creeping into my otherwise fake cheerfulness. After my brush with federal prison and losing the love of my life, just about everything became a hidden dragon waiting behind a door ready to take my fuckin' head off, perhaps even behind the door of a church.

I got up to it, pulled it open halfway and received an assist from a well-formed arm, bare-from-the-puffy-cap-sleeve down. Attached to the arm, an angel-like, twenty-something, blue-eyed redhead in a flowered dress gave me a smile that made itself right at home in my frontal cortex.

"Welcome to the Biscayne Bay Fellowship!" she said. "Come right in and be one with us!"

I had the urge to come back on that one. *"One what?"* Or, *"Oh, sorry. I thought I was in Jim Jones' Church of the Gooey Death."* Or, *"Isn't this the First Credit Card Church of Hialeah?"* I mentally grabbed hold of my runaway brain and shook it until its smart-ass teeth fell out. That kind of so-called humor covered up a sad sack, but now a well-meaning guy on his way back to civilized life.

"Hi!" I dittoed her tone. "I saw your sign, and–"

"You want to meet new friends, or share your story?" she bubbled.

"Uh, both, I think."

"Well, let's start with the first one. I'm Sharon–"

"I hope so." *Ahhh, I didn't say that, did I?*

"What?"

"I mean, I hope to share."

"Let's start over!" she said as she reached down for my hand. I raised mine to meet her in time so as not to look dopey. "Welcome! I'm Sharon Love."

Holy superintendent of trout, I got to tell you, it was hard, super hard for me to hold back what was overpowering my whole frickin' brain, but I banged it down until it looked up at me like a whimpering whipped puppy.

"I'm Joe Oaks, Sharon, and I'm happy to be here."

"You said, you'd like to share?" She kept holding onto my hand.

"Um, yes. I think… yes."

I'll introduce you to our pastor, and he'll call on you at the appropriate time in the program."

"I'd like that, Sharon."

She pulled me by the hand in the direction of a tall, tan, forty-five-ish guy with shiny black hair and ultra white teeth who wrapped up greeting an older couple at the back of the middle aisle and turned to Sharon with me in tow.

"Reverend Good, I have someone for you to meet. This is Joe Oaks!" He and I stuck out our hands and we shook like a couple of guys in a synchronized drill team.

"He said he'd like to share his story with the congregation." Sharon smiled as she switched her eyes from me to him and back to me.

"Of course, Joe. We'd love to hear it." He clasped me on the shoulder with his left hand. "You know, stories of personal redemption motivate others to do the right thing."

I wanted to say, *"Rev, the right thing would be for me to spend a happy weekend holed up with Sharon here,"* but I successfully kicked the line to the curb, and instead said, "I don't claim to be redeemed yet, but I'm getting there."

"Brother, life is a continuous stream of redemption and it keeps getting better!"

Sharon interrupted, "Excuse me. Others are coming in." She returned toward the doublewide front door, and Reverend Good and I took our time watching her reach her destination. I looked back at him again and he was still momentarily fixated on Sharon's posterior perfection. A lesson being that most guys are basically the same.

Reverend Good continued, "I'll call on you at about eleven-thirty. There'll be one woman, Gladys Pippin, who will give her story, and you'll follow her."

I nodded. "Thank you, sir. I'll look forward to it."

The Reverend looked at his watch, nodded back at me, turned and headed down the aisle toward the pulpit.

I wandered down the crimson carpet toward the front, looking left and right until I spotted the best seat. I sat down at the vacant end of a bench about two-thirds toward the front.

A near capacity crowd buzzed with polite conversation, and I began to relax into the warmth of my new adventure.

+++

A crimson curtain opened at exactly eleven o'clock, and revealed twenty-five or so musicians that stood and sat, alert and poised, ready to strike. The leader, erect, with his back to the congregation, tapped his baton three times on the top of a stool and snapped the stick at the air, the band's *go* signal.

Rock and roll to thrill your soul!

I'd never promoted a rock or hip-hop band that sounded more professional. If they didn't have a recording contract, I could sure as hell help 'em find one.

And, here's the biggest little tidbit of all, the choir group behind the musicians rocking out with an arrangement of a new faith song I'd not heard, featured my newest female friend, Sharon Love, the lead singer. Heavenly chops. Well, la-di-dah!

Let's call it divine providence.

Hey, we're all rollin' in the deep, right?

Joe Oaks

ARC
PUBLISHERS

We hope you enjoyed Hot Scores,
the first episode of Joe Oaks' misadventures.
Another, *Heavenly Chops,* is next,
and there are ten more to follow.

If you have also read
Bud Connell's award-winning thriller,
Peak Experience: A Novel,
(available at Amazon.com,
BarnesandNobel.com, TowerBooks.com
and on Amazon's Kindle)
the second in the series, *Ultima,*
featuring more memorable characters
and some of the originals,
will be published and also available
within the calendar year.

Bud Connell's books
are periodically available to be downloaded
from the Kindle Owner's Lending Library,
free-of-charge to Amazon Prime Members.

All Bud Connell-authored books
may be obtained from most on-line retailers
and for most electronic devices using Kindle apps,
which also may be downloaded free-of-charge.

About the Author

Bud Connell was successful in several careers before becoming a novelist. His background in media, business, and entertainment prepared him to create stories and characters with wide appeal and high entertainment value. With each new book, he is becoming a recognized voice in fiction.

His first novel, Peak Experience, a thriller with prolific servings of intrigue, suspense, and romance, has won several national awards, and remains on various bestseller lists, while staying within the top three to ten percent of Amazon Kindle downloads.

Watch for new offerings by Author Bud Connell; and for frequently updated information, you're invited to join him on Facebook or BudConnell.com.

Thank you for reading

HOT SCORES

A Joe Oaks Novel

JoeOaks.com